LEAP OF FAITH

A ROMANCE NOVEL

Pam Kelly

LEAP OF FAITH

This book is a work of fiction. Names, characters, businesses, organizations, places, events, and incidents either are the product of the author's research or imagination or are used fictitiously. Any resemblance to actual persons, living or dead, or events, is entirely coincidental.

ISBN: 978-0-9801502-3-0 (paperback)
ISBN: 978-0-9801502-4-7 (ebook)

Editor: Hilda R. Davis, Ph.D. (HildaRDavis.com)
Cover Design: Mary Ann Smith (Reedsy.com)
Formatting by Polgarus Studio (PolgarusStudio.com)

For my parents, Jewel and Mattie Frierson
They were the first to teach me about unconditional love,
the ups and downs of marriage,
and the true meaning of 'in sickness and in health'

With many thanks and much love to:

The people at the Writespace workshop who, after hearing a few pages from the first short story version, were excited and wanted to know what happened, and encouraged me to complete the story;

The family and friends who became beta readers of the short story version because I knew I could count on their honesty and detailed feedback:
Terry Bass-Belle, Beverly Franklin,
Mea Freeman, and Lori Perkins;

Gerry, a loyal government employee who helped me understand the real workings of agency operations;

Hilda R. Davis, who turned a chance meeting at a writing conference into friendship/sisterhood/family and who started as a beta reader but became my editor extraordinaire, master motivator and chief cheer leader who encouraged me to see the writing as a gift and to follow wherever it leads;

Everyone who believes in the possibilities of romance and love;

and everyone who reads this book!

Blessings and Grace to you all!

CHAPTER ONE

It was a night of celebration for Robert McKnight and his twin sister Rochelle, their fortieth birthday, and Willie G's Seafood was their restaurant of choice this year. It was upscale but not stuffy, with three sections to choose from: one with white tablecloths, one where the hardwood tables had no tablecloths, and a long, fully stocked bar with seating that separated the two sections.

As they pulled up to the valet, Robert got a call from his business partners so he asked his family to go on inside and be seated, saying he would only be a minute. He stood across from the valet stand to have the conversation, watching as cars pulled up and guests got out. It was a popular place.

His partners were teasing him about being old when a silver Lexus pulled up and the prettiest caramel colored legs he had seen in a while stepped out in iridescent heels, followed by a short straight black skirt and purple blouse and jacket. She looked to be about five feet nine inches tall in the heels. When he saw her face he told his partners he had to call them back.

She had a head full of dark brown curly hair framing a heart shaped face. Her eyes were light brown and almond shaped, over a small pointed nose and perfectly shaped lips, with a pointed cupids bow in the center of her top lip and the slightest pout in her bottom lip. She looked sexy and sweet and cuddly all rolled into one. His mouth watered and his body went on full alert.

As she got out of the car, her phone rang causing her to reach back in for her purse and turn her back to him to answer. All of a sudden she started squealing and stomping her feet and jumping up and down in excitement. He immediately wondered what he would have to do to make her squeal like that for him.

When she hung up and turned to give the valet her key, Robert and the pretty lady made eye contact. She was still smiling and he noticed deep dimples in both cheeks. Robert loved a lady with dimples. To him they were sexy and fun to kiss. Then he distinctly heard that still small voice letting him know he had just seen the woman he had been looking for during the day and praying for in the wee hours of some very lonely nights. A woman to love and share his complicated life. In his heart, he wanted to believe it was God, but in his head, he said no, it was too weird. At a restaurant? Without even talking to her? He needed more than a pretty face. He had been with lots of pretty faces but they had no substance. He needed someone to talk with, who enjoyed conversations on a variety of topics. Someone who liked to have fun. Someone smart, a challenge even.

Then he heard his mothers' voice in his head, "This is your blessing baby." Those words gave him pause because she only said them when he was getting something good that he had not expected. Now he was really excited and ready to see what would unfold.

He quickly moved toward the door so he could be in place to open it and engage her in conversation. When she got there, he looked directly at her and smiled, then said, "Good evening. It sounds like you just got some exciting news. Care to share?"

Before responding she paused, assessing this handsome man who held the door for her. He was about six feet tall, solidly built, not an ounce of fat. Muscular. Toned. Smooth milk chocolate skin was the backdrop for his black hair, thick eyebrows, slender nose and full lips. When he smiled, she saw the prettiest white teeth and two very deep dimples in his cheeks. She inhaled his very captivating scent, a woodsy cologne with hints of mandarin orange and jasmine. Visions of licking his skin danced in her head and she imagined that he would taste as good as he smelled.

"It is very good news. I'm a writer and my new agent just got me a deal for two books. That's like winning the lottery. It's a dream come true." She couldn't help but smile.

"Congratulations! That is fantastic news. I'm happy for you." He was very sincere and she could feel it. "Are you meeting someone here?" he asked, hoping that she would say no.

"No, I was just coming in for a quick drink then be on my way home."

The host interrupted their conversation to get them seated, giving the pretty lady the opportunity to say to

Robert "Have a good evening" and go to the ladies room. She needed to collect her thoughts, first to dance another minute in the excitement about the book deal and then to think about this man she had just encountered. Somehow, she knew they would have another moment together and she wanted to be calm and ready.

He was clearly a man of means judging by his clothes, which looked expensive and were tailor made for his very nice body. He was confident but didn't seem cocky. Most men who looked like him were so into themselves, you were just an accessory to make them look good and you could see it immediately in their approach to you. His direct look made her believe he was really listening and wanted to hear what she had to say. But men like him had more than their share of women and she did not want to be 'one of many' because that's not who she was or wanted to be.

As Robert headed to the table where his family was seated, he watched the pretty lady go in the direction of the ladies room and noticed that she and the bartender waved and smiled at each other as she passed by. He wondered if she was a regular at the bar or if they were flirting or in a relationship. He would soon find out.

Robert's sister Shelly always asked for a table with an extra seat for her purse so there was already a chair available for the pretty lady if he could get her to join them. He knew he was attractive and charming to many women so he never had a shortage of female attention coming at him. This was different. He wanted *her* attention, starting tonight. He wanted to know more about her background and what her thoughts and dreams were and what she wanted in a man. No woman had interested him like this in a long, long time. He told his family he would be right back and headed toward the bar area, on a mission to get her to have dinner with them.

CHAPTER TWO

When she came out of the ladies room, Robert was waiting for her in the alcove, leaning against the doorframe. His heart was beating rapidly. He held out his right hand to introduce himself and she put her right hand in his. He covered hers with his left hand and held on while they spoke. He looked into her eyes. "Hi. I'm Robert McKnight but my family calls me Bobby." His hands were big and warm and made her feel safe, protected.

She responded in a soft voice and a curious look, wondering what else he would say. "Hi. I'm Patricia Harris."

He would not let her hand go and just looked at her with a smile. "You are a beautiful woman Patricia Harris, and it is a pleasure to meet you. Your hands are warm," he said.

"Well thank you. Your hands are warm too. And big" she said, looking in his eyes and returning the compliment while trying to keep her tone casual and light.

In that moment, as they gazed at one another, they both felt an energy pass between them, an electric pulse that signaled a sense of excitement and anticipation. She was surprised and pulled back ever so slightly. He felt it too, and was amused that she was trying to pull away. He was determined to continue holding her hand and to keep her from disconnecting with him. She could feel a warm sensation start to envelope her body and knew immediately that something very different was about to happen. It felt like she was having an out of body experience. Or about to faint. Either way she knew it was a turning point in her life.

He finally responded to her. "Yes," he said, "I'm a big guy. Everything about me is big. Will that be a problem for you?" He continued to hold her hand and look at her, waiting for a response.

She played it cool, laughed, and said, "I don't know what that means, but I do know that you need to be careful. The last man who held my hand like this ended up being my husband."

"Oh?" He looked for a wedding ring and seeing none asked, "Well where is he now?" "Dead," she responded.

"Oh. Well has anyone taken his place?" he asked, wanting to know if she had married again or if she was seeing anyone.

"Not yet" she confessed.

He responded quietly, nodding with self-assurance, "OK. I will."

"Will what?" she queried with a slight frown, wondering what kind of lame line he would come up with. She had heard quite a few, from 'I'll keep your bed warm for you now' to 'I'll take care of your honey-do list' to 'I'll pay all your bills.' She was never interested.

"Marry you." He had stopped smiling but continued to look directly into her eyes.

She was caught off guard. That was a new line and totally unexpected. Few men want to talk marriage, even after being in a relationship for a while. She gave him points for originality and boldness, but it was still a line.

"Sure, okay," she said flippantly, pulling hard to disengage her hand and step around him to signal the end of the conversation. But he was not done and continued to hold on to her hand.

"Until then may I have the pleasure of celebrating your good news with you? Will you join me and my family for dinner, drinks, Champagne, whatever you want?"

"You are kind, Robert, but I would not want to intrude upon your time with your family." She tried to pull her hand away but again he held on.

"Actually" he pressed, "you would not be intruding. Today is my birthday. My twin sister Shelly's and mine. You would be joining our celebration. In fact, with your new book deal we can celebrate it all together. Better than celebrating alone don't you think?"

He started rubbing the back of her hand. "It would be a fantastic birthday gift for me. And who knows, our being together tonight might give you something to write about in one of your books." His eyes were piercing in their directness, but soft and warm in their gaze.

Sexiness was radiating out of him from every pore and she was absorbing every ray of heat. All parts of her were engaged: the giggly school girl; the teen heartbeat of a first love; the grown and sexy 'I am woman in need of a real man' all flooded her soul.

She took another look at Robert McKnight. They looked at each other for about thirty seconds and she could feel the blanket of heat wrap completely around her. Now *her* heart was beating hard. And fast.

She finally looked back down at their hands still together. It had been a powerful few minutes, but she wasn't sure what she wanted to do.

In her heart and in her spirit she heard God say, 'here he is…the one you've been begging me for, the one on your vision board, the one true love you say you need to make your great life complete.'

She opened her mouth to speak but nothing came out so she shook her head no.

CHAPTER THREE

She tried to pull away again but he kept holding on. Robert could tell she had mixed feelings so he made the decision for her. Still holding her hand, he said, "Come meet my family. We love to read but we don't know any writers so it would be fun for them to meet you. It will only take a moment."

He guided her to the table and made introductions: "Family, this is Patricia Harris and she is a writer. Ms. Harris, this is my sister Rochelle Baldwin. We call her Shelly and she's a nurse. This is my brother-in-law minister and construction manager Tommy, Rev. Thomas Baldwin Sr.; and this young man is my ten-year-old nephew TJ, short for Thomas Jr."

They were curious when Robert arrived at the table holding a woman's hand. He rarely had women join them for dinner, and never for their birthday, so they wondered who she was and what Robert was doing. Tommy, Shelly, and TJ said hello, looking at her then at Robert then back at her. Robert's eyes were focused on her.

"Please, call me Pat. It is very nice to meet all of you! And Happy Birthday to you both." She smiled at Shelly and Robert.

Robert then shared Pat's good news. "She just got a two book deal and I'm trying to get her to have dinner and celebrate with us." They all said yes, invited her to stay, and expressed their excitement for her. Tommy asked her what type of books she wrote, and when she said contemporary romance, Shelly became very animated, moving her purse, and asking Pat, "Here, sit next to me so we can talk. I am a huge romance reader." Pat tried to protest, saying she would be intruding but they all assured her that she was welcome.

Pat looked at Robert who was holding the chair out for her. She gave him a smirk that let him know that she recognized how he used his family to get his way. Truth was she wanted to stay. She had no one to go home to so being out with new people would be a welcome change and she liked that they shared in her joy. He commented quietly, "See, that wasn't so bad, was it?"

"Well played Mr. McKnight," Pat whispered with a smile as she took her seat.

The female server came to take their drink orders and everyone noticed how close she stood to Robert, and how she asked him a couple of times if there was anything else he needed. Robert was used to the attention so he was polite in answering but did not engage her or tease her into thinking he was paying her any special attention.

Pat watched the server and Robert's reaction and appreciated the way he handled the overtures the server was making. She also took a good look at the family as they gave their orders. Robert and Shelly looked like identical twins with the warm chocolate skin, jet black hair, thick eyebrows and dimples. Shelly was as feminine and beautiful with a head full of long hair and a shapely body as Robert was handsome and sexy with short cut hair and muscles. Tommy was also a warm brown color but he was tall and slender with a bald head, round dark eyes, a broad nose and full but not thick lips. TJ looked like Robert and Shelly in his face and his dark thick hair but was slender like his dad.

After the server left, Shelly launched into a series of questions, asking Pat, "Why did you become a writer? Why romance books? Who are your favorite writers? And can we talk about why so few men read romance novels? They know they should for good tips on how to be romantic."

Pat was both amused and flattered by her enthusiasm then responded to the first two questions. "I've always had a vivid imagination and dreams about people and relationships. They used to frighten me until I got older and began to understand that most were not dreams of harm. They were more about how people showed they loved each other and things they would do for each other. In high school, I started writing short stories about the dreams and my English teachers were very supportive, saying that I had a nice writing style. I took journalism and creative writing in college and decided to see what a writing career could look like. I still have to have a day job, so I work in a bookstore. Over the last few years, I've published articles about theories on romance and a few novellas. I used them as a calling card to get an agent for my first full length book."

"And look at God," Shelly responded. "You have a two book deal. Now that this dream has come true, what else is on your bucket list?"

"The usual stuff I write about," Pat said laughing. "Love, marriage, the happily ever after. You kind of get caught up when you're writing about the same thing all the time." She looked around the table as she spoke but stayed focused on Shelly for the last part, not wanting Robert to think she was throwing hints.

Robert and Tommy looked at each other and smiled. TJ was into the games on his phone so he was not paying attention. Robert listened attentively to how Pat talked about her work. He liked her expressiveness and excitement and the way she spoke with respect to his sister and her questions.

Before Pat could answer Shelly's questions on favorite writers and why men don't read romance, the server came with the drinks and took their dinner orders. Pat ordered the chopped salad and organic Chicken; Robert ordered the Chicken and Sausage Gumbo, salad, and Wild Salmon, saying he had missed lunch in order to get to Houston on time for dinner so he was starving; Shelly ordered the salad and Grilled Shrimp; Tommy wanted the eight ounce Filet Mignon with a salad; and TJ asked for the Gumbo and a piece of his dad's steak.

Pat took the opportunity to shift the conversation to the family and ask questions to get to know them. "Why nursing?" she asked Shelly.

Shelly responded proudly, "Like mother, like daughter."

Tommy's response to "Why ministry?" was a bit

more involved. "I felt the call in high school after growing up in church and was active in the youth programs. Helping neighbors or family was my choice for service. I was always chosen to be a speaker at church programs. The pulpit felt like the place where I was supposed to give voice to my messages to help and to serve. I am an associate pastor at Wheeler Avenue Baptist Church so I get to preach every now and then and I oversee the Congregational Care and Outreach ministries. It's the best of both worlds."

Pat liked kids and wanted to get to know TJ so she included him in the questions to the family. "Hey TJ. I'll bet you're not doing homework on your phone. Is that a video game or a movie?" TJ looked up quickly from his phone to give her a polite response. "A video game." Pat commented back to him, "I don't know anything about those, so can I ask you another question?" He kept looking down but nodded yes. She asked, "What are your favorite things about your mom, dad, and uncle?" He looked up to see her looking at him, waiting for his answer. He liked that she really wanted to have a conversation with him, like his Uncle Bobby talked to him, so he put the phone on the table and became very animated and engaged.

"My mom is a great cook. She's pretty and fun. All my friends like to come to our house because there is always something good to eat and music playing. We dance a lot and we play lots of games. She treats them like family, always talking to them, asking about their parents and school and their grades. She makes sure we have their favorite snack when they come over and she always makes them a cake for their birthday. They love her."

Pat asked him if he minded sharing her with them since he is an only child but he said no and laughed. "They have to go home and I get her all to myself again." Shelly looked at him with motherly pride and said she never knew any of that, surprised at all that TJ noticed.

TJ's favorite thing about his dad? He was beaming when he shared, "He helps me with my homework and comes to all of my games. I play a lot of sports. First it was Little League baseball, now basketball and soccer, and I run track. And my dad helps me and my friends work on our plays in the backyard or in the park every week.

"Uncle Bobby comes to see me every month when it's not tax season so we can hang out, just me and him." TJ was grinning at Robert, clearly proud that Robert took a lot of time with him and treated him like a young man, not a kid. "We do all kinds of cool stuff. We go to the zoo and aquarium, food festivals, and baseball and basketball and football games. If my grades are good, especially all A's, he takes me shopping.

"Everybody says we look alike so they think he's my dad when we're out, especially the ladies who are always trying to talk to him. He does not let them bother us though. He says our time is special and we have to be polite but firm to make them leave us alone. He says he's giving me lessons on handling the girls but I don't like girls like that." They all laughed at that one.

The salads and Gumbo came and while the dishes

were being passed out a curious Pat turned to Robert to ask, "So what about you Mr. McKnight? What's your story? You don't live here in Houston?"

"No, I live in Dallas. I'm an accountant and have a business there with two friends. I come here about once a month, usually on Friday and stay until Sunday to spend time with my family."

"Oh," Pat said, her tone sounding a little disappointed.

"Do you have a problem with long distance relationships?" he asked her.

Pat thought for a moment, flipping back through her relationship history, and then responded, "Honestly I've never had one so I don't know."

"How would you feel about moving to Dallas?" He had a feeling that would be a problem.

"Never thought about it. Never had a reason to." She was very casual in her response.

"Well now you do." He looked directly at her when he said it, then winked.

"And what else do I need to know about you since you say you're going to be my next husband? What qualities do you have that would convince me to say yes?" Pat was curious. She really wanted to know more, not because she had thoughts of marrying him, but because he was sexy and quiet, watchful, not trying to dominate the conversation. He intrigued her.

He laughed. "Convince you, huh? Okay, I'll take a shot. I'm a nerd who likes numbers and I like to read but I also like to have fun. Like TJ said, we dance and play games and go out to enjoy life. I take care of my finances so I can live a decent life. I prefer quality over quantity in people and most things. I am fiercely loyal to family and close friends. I like to stay on top of current events and have been known to engage in a debate or two about people, politics, or business. I am a Christian but have not found a church home in Dallas yet. And I am ready to get married and eventually have children." Pat watched him as he spoke, believing that though his tone was lighthearted, he was sincere and honest.

When the servers left, Tommy said grace and the focus shifted to the food.

Robert asked, Pat if she had ever tried the Gumbo and when she said no, he took her spoon and dipped it into his bowl, making sure to get a piece of chicken and a piece of sausage, then leaned over to put the spoon to her lips. Their eyes met. It felt very sensual to be fed by a man like that and she knew a blush was coming. Pat licked her lips and opened her mouth to let him slide the spoon in. He watched her lick her lips, following her tongue, then looked back into her eyes. His body got very warm and he whispered, "Mmm. I think I just had dessert." She looked down, very sure that she was into full blush mode. When she tasted the Gumbo, they both moaned quietly. Robert asked "Good huh?" She nodded yes, and he said, looking at her lips again, "for me too." He didn't mean the Gumbo and she knew it. They looked at each other and both chuckled. Tommy and Shelly heard the moans and looked at Pat and Robert then each other. Both wondered if Robert and Pat were headed to a 'hook-up' or if they were witnessing the start of a real life romance.

CHAPTER FOUR

The entrees were hot and seasoned to perfection. Everyone was happy with his or her selections but everybody's plate was fair game for sharing, especially the seafood and steak. That's why everyone ordered a different dish on the menu. It was a family thing so they would know what to order next time they visited the restaurant. Robert even ate some chicken off Pat's plate so she would not feel left out since she said she didn't eat seafood and very little steak. Plus he wanted an excuse to keep her attention.

As they were finishing dinner, Tommy commented that it was Pat's turn to share. "You know about us, now tell us more about you."

Pat was happy to oblige. Robert and his family were kind and fun. It felt natural to be with them. She gave them the short version. "I'm a Chicagoan, born and bred, an only child who grew up with loving parents. I went away to undergrad and grad school then came right back home to be with them. I'm glad I did because both of them died within five years of each other. My dad died first. Just before my mom died I got married. I wanted her to know that I had someone to love me and I would be okay. Or so I thought. My mom died, then not long after my marriage died too.

"But I am still in good hands. I have aunts and uncles who treat me like one of their own, and cousins that I grew up with who are more like my brothers and sisters. That's one of the reasons I moved here. My dad's only brother married one of my mom's sisters — that's a story for another time — and they moved to Houston because of his job.

When my marriage died, I wanted to be close to family and Uncle Roy and Aunt Ginny asked me to move to Houston. I was tired of the cold and snow anyway so it was an easy decision."

Shelly asked, "Do you have any children?

"Not yet." Pat responded with a smile and a wink at TJ. "Maybe I'll get lucky one day and have a nice young man like TJ." TJ smiled back at her. He liked Uncle Bobby's new friend.

Tommy asked if she was a Christian. "Yes. I was raised in a Baptist church but have not yet affiliated with one in Houston. I have visited your church, Wheeler Avenue, and a few others but not settled on one."

Robert asked Pat if she was ready to get married again. It felt like a loaded question given what he had said earlier, by the restroom, about marrying her. Before Pat could answer, one of the deacons of Wheeler came over to say hello to Tommy and the family. Thank you God, Pat said very quietly under her breath.

After dinner, Robert laced his fingers together with Pat's under the table and his thumb was rubbing the back of her hand. Pat looked down at their hands resting on his leg then up at his face. He looked at her and whispered, "I like holding your hand. I also like the questions you ask, the way your mind works."

Robert was getting a lot of attention from various women as they passed by the table. The female manager came over to make sure everything was good, looking only at him. He knew what was happening but kept his eyes focused on Pat and his family when he answered her.

When Pat commented about his 'fan club,' he said casually, "It happens, but I'm pretty good at ignoring them though I try not to be rude. Will this be a problem for you? For us?" he asked.

Pat looked around and thought about it for a moment before answering and finally said, "As long as your attention is always on me, we can work through it. You have to manage the aggressive ones or I will. When you or your attention strays, I'm out. I don't compete. I believe you should be happy with whomever you want and it's your job to make sure it's always me."

He listened carefully to her response then said, "Understood. I'm good with that."

As Tommy paid the check, Pat gathered her purse and jacket and began to say good night. They all said at the same time, "Not yet. Join us for dessert." Tommy explained, "Shelly has baked a cake for their birthday, a tradition their mom started when they were young and Shelly continues. It is waiting at our home only twenty minutes away."

She protested in earnest. "Thank you for allowing me

to share this birthday celebration with you! I have intruded long enough and want you to enjoy the rest of your evening with just the family. Robert and I will stay in touch so I hope to see you again."

Shelly and Tommy looked at each other then at Robert as Shelly said, "We have enjoyed getting to know you and having dinner with you. We really should finish the evening together with dessert."

Pat didn't know what to say. She wanted to go with them, but instead told them, "You are very kind, but my mother taught me not to overstay my welcome with people so that they would be happy to see me when I come around again. It feels like this is the right time to leave tonight."

Robert asked Pat to sit for a minute and wait for him to walk his family to the door. He gave them the valet ticket to his car and asked them to go on to the house, saying he would be there shortly.

CHAPTER FIVE

When he got back to the table, Robert began to share his life and his heart: "I told you I live in Dallas so I'm only here for a couple of days. In fact, I came in a day early this time because of our birthday dinner. On Saturdays, I spend the day hanging out with TJ. That just leaves tomorrow for us to spend time together and maybe Saturday night. I usually leave early on Sunday to try to beat some of the traffic.

"When I saw you outside, I heard God say 'there she is, the one you've been praying for to love and love you.' This has never happened to me before so I am extremely interested to find out what He has in store for us. I don't date a lot, but I have been looking for the right woman to come along that I could marry. I hope you got to know me and my family well enough tonight to trust that we are good people and you will be safe."

He paused for a moment, allowing his comments to sink in, then asked, "So Ms. Harris, will you make my birthday complete by joining us for dessert?" He was serious and his eyes were very focused, never leaving hers. He held her hands the whole time too.

His look made her want to run away as quickly as

possible, but at the same time she wanted to say yes to anything he wanted. She protested again, realizing that if she went for dessert she would not be able to resist him for anything else. She would be all in. She felt she couldn't risk it. If this was something special then she needed to go home and think clearly and let him miss her like all the good dating books say.

He could see the angst in her face as she pulled away from him. He persisted: "Remember Tommy is a pastor so he does not tolerate irresponsible behavior. And none of us will let TJ see us do inappropriate things. I promise you will be ok. What can I do to assure you that nothing bad will happen to you?"

She thought to herself that she really liked getting to know him and his family and she felt safe with them. He persuaded her with that final appeal.

Pat sent a text to her Aunt Ginny with Robert's name and phone number and Shelly and Tommy's name and address. It was a safety measure her aunt and uncle asked for when she was going out with men they had not met.

She explained to Robert, "They just want to be able to find me if anything came up or, heaven forbid, I went missing. I appreciate it and always comply. It is a security measure for me too, letting men know that I am not alone in this world."

When they got to the valet, Robert revealed that he needed to ride to the house with her because he had driven the family to the restaurant in his car and they had taken it home.

She frowned at him. "You were mighty sure of

yourself that I would come with you. What if I had said no?"

He gave her his most apologetic look and stepped back before responding. "Then I would call an Uber or Lyft. I would not force myself or my family on you. I thought we had a connection and you would be willing to spend a little more time with us. I'm sorry if I offended you. Does this mean you changed your mind?"

Pat looked upset and said, "I don't like it when people make assumptions about me. Especially when you don't know me. I can see that you are handsome and charming Mr. McKnight, but that is not always enough. Respect is important. I am not one of your groupies. I'll drop you off."

The ride to Shelly and Tommy's house was tense and quiet, except for the GPS giving directions. Pat was wondering why men always thought you wanted them and would fall for their antics instead of being straightforward. Robert was looking at her as she drove, trying to figure out what to say to keep her from leaving as soon as they got to Shelly and Tommy's. He had become even more interested in her as the evening progressed and he was not ready to write this one off as bad timing or saying the wrong thing.

When they pulled up in front of the house Robert apologized again. "I really did not intend to disrespect you. You are definitely not a groupie. I knew you were different, special when I saw you, and listening to you this evening has been a joy. You are fun and smart and refreshing. Blame me for being excited about getting to spend more time with you before I leave Houston. I haven't wanted to spend a lot of time with any one woman in forever so I did not handle this well. I'm sorry."

Tommy and TJ were outside checking the sprinklers. TJ ran to the car to tell them that his mom was waiting and wanted to know what toppings they wanted on their cake. Robert told him to give them a minute. Tommy could see that Pat and Robert were looking in different directions and the mood had shifted since the restaurant so he steered TJ into the house. Robert got out of the passenger side and walked around to Pat on the driver's side, unsure if he was going to help her out of the car or say goodnight. Either way he still wanted to see her again.

"This has been a really fun evening Patricia Harris. I would very much like to spend more time with you. Do you play Monopoly?" Robert was anxious for her to come in and thought of a fun analogy.

Pat nodded yes but was still looking straight ahead, not at him. Robert pressed her, "Then can you give me one get out of jail free card for tonight and come in with us for cake? Please?"

Pat realized that by not going in the family would wonder what happened and she liked them too much to come off as bitchy. And she didn't want to be the cause of a crappy moment in the middle of a very nice birthday celebration, so she got out of the car.

A big grin appeared on Robert's face and he exhaled a huge sigh of relief, shouting "Thank You!" and pulled her into a bear hug. Pat rolled her eyes and followed him into the house. Truth be told she was happy too. She liked Robert and his family. Maybe she shouldn't be quick to judge on the first day meeting him.

The house was beautiful, warm, and cozy, just like the family who lived there. It was a two story, French country style, decorated with modern country furnishings, lots of wood beams and wood tables, fabrics that were soft and colorful but durable. High quality and beautiful, but you could get comfortable and not panic if you spilled something. Pat was very complimentary. "This house is gorgeous! And it feels like love and fun family times happen here. I don't feel that in some of the houses I've been in."

A proud and beaming Shelly gave Pat the tour of the first floor. The family room, kitchen, office, master, and another bedroom and bath called Robert's Room, were downstairs. He had casual and business clothes, shoes, and toiletries there so he never had to pack much if at all when he came to visit. There were family photos everywhere so she got to see plenty of pictures of Shelly and Robert as they were growing up and how much they looked like their mom.

Shelly called up to TJ to let him know they were coming upstairs so Pat could see the rest of the house. He had his own suite—two bedrooms, a game room with a large sectional sofa, a 60" flat screen television, and a full bathroom with double sinks in the vanity. When they got to the top of the stairs, Pat asked TJ for a tour. He was proud to show off his sports themed décor, his bedroom with his trophies, and his combination "office/playroom" where he did his homework and had a table set up for puzzles and games and toys. Pat and TJ were talking and laughing as if they had known each other a long time so Shelly eased back downstairs to let them bond and get dessert ready.

The 7Up pound cake Shelly made had glaze all over it. Pat jumped right in to help in the kitchen, getting spoons and napkins while Shelly cut and plated the cake and ice cream. Pat noticed as she moved around that TJ was right; their pantry, fridge, and freezer were well stocked with food, fruit, and snacks, including a variety of ice cream and frozen yogurt flavors. They all sat around the large island and continued to talk about the family as they ate.

Pat asked her favorite questions for all couples: "How did you meet? How did you know he or she was the one?"

Shelly glowed like most people do. She was proud to tell the story of how she and Tommy met in college, in the library. "We saw each other there almost every day for two weeks before Tommy got up the nerve to ask me out on a date. He said he was intimidated because so many people were always around me, and he assumed I had a boyfriend."

They were together every day thereafter, meeting for meals and their library sessions, and dating on a budget. They both knew they had fallen in love when they went home for Christmas break (her to Houston, him to Milwaukee) and stayed on the phone with each other for twelve straight hours. Neither one wanted to hang up, but her dad finally intervened. He told Tommy that if he was going to take up that much of his daughters' time then he needed to come to Houston and present himself to the family. And so he did.

Shelly continued telling the story: "Dad interrogated him for two hours about his family background, his habits, his values, his plans for the future, and what his intentions and plans were for his precious daughter."

Tommy added his perspective. "He was a tough interrogator The McKnight's were very particular about who their children partnered with so I was thrilled to finally get their approval. Even Bobby was on board. I thought he would be much harder on me because he and Shelly are so close, and she had told me that he never liked any of her boyfriends. I understood why Bobby was so careful not to bring anybody around that wasn't special or couldn't fit in, which makes it interesting that you two just met this evening and you've already had dinner with us."

Pat turned to look at Robert and he looked back at her with a deadpan look on his face and said, loud enough for everyone to hear, "Yes, I already believe you are special."

Pat felt those heat waves radiating down her body, and hoped that she was not turning red again.

Robert was relaxed and enjoyed watching how Pat engaged with his family and how they responded so warmly to her and her questions. His chair was very close to Pat's, which made their thighs touch.

Robert had a great sense of humor and laughed with pride at the stories Shelly and Tommy told. He added his own perspective. "I liked that Tommy stood up to the interrogation without flinching or trying to run away. He kept his eyes on Shelly the whole time, looking like a love struck puppy. We were impressed at his focus and dedication to her. I thought he was a bit nerdy, but that was ok. I was a nerd. I could see that he was good for her too, because while he was nice and attentive to her, he would not let her push him around even though she was always trying to get her way."

Shelly and Tommy looked at each other and laughed. Tommy commented, "She's still trying to get her way. Sometimes I have to reign her in." Smiling, Shelly said, "Hey, it's been working for almost twenty years. I have no complaints."

The Baldwin's were clearly a good match and a very happy family.

When Pat asked about their childhood and what it was like growing up as twins, Shelly gave her take first.

"Our personalities were strong at an early age. As we got older it was fun to always have someone my age to hang out with even though he was my brother and really stubborn."

Robert laughed and said, "Shelly was always trying to boss me around, saying she was the oldest so I had to do what she said."

Shelly chose to clarify, "But that only worked when he wanted to do what I was asking him to do anyway. All the other times he just ignored me and did what he wanted to do. He was no pushover. He wasn't defiant just to show me that I couldn't tell him what to do. It was more like he knew as much as I did about what should be done so I didn't need to tell him anything."

"And he was the hot guy in high school. The girls always liked him. He was handsome, polite, smart— always carrying a bunch of books and reading. And he was a jock. A geek but cool. I had more than a few girlfriends who just wanted to hang out with me so they could see him but he paid them no attention."

Robert reminded her, "My friends came to see you too." He rolled his eyes and told how "Every season, whatever sport I played, when the guys on the team found out we had to clean the house every Saturday before I could go anywhere, most of them came over to help. Shelly and I always had a good laugh about how goofy they acted when she came into a room. I don't think she ever dated any of them."

Pat finally asked about their parents thinking that they might live out of town since they were not at the restaurant for the birthday celebration. Shelly and Robert looked at each other with sadness and said at the same time, "they died."

"I'm very sorry to hear that." Pat said softly.

Robert and Shelly paused to reflect for just a moment then Robert volunteered to share a 'fun fact' with Pat — that their first names came from their parents' middle names: Savannah Rochelle and Jonathan Robert McKnight.

It was getting late and TJ still had homework to do so he went up to his room while the adults collected the dishes and cleaned the table. Pat gathered her things to go. Robert leaned over to whisper in her ear, "Don't leave me."

She whispered back, "Robert it's been a long day for me and I've been with you and your family all evening. I need to go home. We can talk tomorrow."

He leaned in close and said again, "Please don't leave. Not now."

Pat protested again. "Robert, come on. I stayed for dinner and came here for dessert. Your family needs to go to bed and I need to go home and do the same."

This time he spoke very softly in her ear: "I don't want you to leave. Not now. Not ever. Marry me Patricia Harris."

"What?" She wasn't sure she heard him correctly.

His next words shocked her but they were loud and clear. "Marry me. Tonight. Right now. On my birthday. Tommy can do the ceremony."

Shelly and Tommy stopped moving and looked at each other. Then they all looked at Robert like he was insane.

Pat was speechless, then finally said, "you don't know me to ask me that."

"No pre-nup?" Shelly asked with a look of terror on her face.

Tommy asked, "Why the rush? What is going on with you? You know you need to get a marriage license first and wait 72 hours before you can get married in the state of Texas?"

CHAPTER SIX

Robert looked directly at Pat as he shared with Tommy and Shelly that he heard God say that Pat was 'the one,' their discussion by the bathroom, and their talk after the family left the restaurant. He did not want to wait, so they would do the steps out of order: have the ceremony tonight and get the license on tomorrow, Friday.

Tommy and Shelly knew Robert to be a very serious man, a no-nonsense guy, taking very well thought out, calculated risks in his life so they saw his behavior and proposal as unusual, but probably not as far-fetched as they might be for someone more practical. They could see something special happening between Robert and Pat at the restaurant almost immediately but didn't want to say anything. They were actually persuaded.

Then they all looked at Pat. She laughed nervously as she backed out of the kitchen and took a few steps toward the family room heading to the front door. Robert caught her in the family room, wrapping his arms around her. She couldn't help but inhale his scent. She could hardly breathe. He asked if they could sit on the sofa and talk.

Tommy and Shelly went to their bedroom to give Pat

and Robert some privacy and discuss this turn of events. They announced that they were not going to bed so if they decided to have the ceremony, knock on their door.

Pat was very nervous and tended to be very talkative when she get that way so she started the conversation. "Robert, I'm flattered. Really. And to be honest, of course I am attracted to you, like most of the other women who saw you tonight. But I just met you! You seem like a great guy and your family is delightful but marriage? You clearly don't need to do this to get women so what's going on with you?

Robert responded, "Patricia, I have never been married before. I have never even asked another woman to marry me. But I want to be married now and I am ready to be married. I am ready to love you and promise to be a great husband."

"You probably will make a great husband," she countered. "But I've been married before, and not all that long ago. I have been wooed and fooled by attraction, personality, and promises. You know that old saying 'once burned twice shy?' That's me. I am too fragile right now to take a chance again. I don't need to put my issues and insecurities on you. Plus I am afraid of what loving you would require of me. You have a lot of women who find you handsome and sexy and are not shy about telling you. How often can you say no? I don't compete. Or share."

Robert was not to be denied, offering an unexpected response: "Let me tell you something that not many people know: I am celibate. Have been for almost two years. Maybe if I explain why it will help you understand me better and put my desire to marry you in context."

"Celibacy was a moral choice for me, a decision to be a better man," he responded, very quietly and seriously. "Before my folks died I was living the life. Had a good job, bought a condo, and was dating with an eye toward marriage in about ten or fifteen years. Had a couple of relationships that lasted a few months or so but they weren't the forever kind of love. I kept dating around."

"After my folks died, I only looked to women to help me cope. I wasn't even dating as much as using women for sex to give me momentary relief from grief. None of them mattered to me. They only served to keep me from facing reality. I was in a lot of pain and should have reached out for help in therapy, not in women's beds like I was a player, something I have never been. After a while I realized my life was out of control, that I was probably hurting some feelings in the process. I'm sure one or two of the ladies would have wanted to work toward something serious with me but I was not interested. That was not right. It was selfish and not who I had developed myself to be as a man.

"What I was missing was real love, the love of a good woman, a woman I could give all of the pent up love I had in me. I needed to stop being reckless and start to rely on God again. So I asked Him to heal my heart and mind and prepare me for the woman I could love.

"That's when I knew I needed to cleanse my life from the inappropriate things I had been doing and present myself again to God. So I became celibate and Tommy helped me renew my baptismal vows. It was only then that I started having some peace and allowed God to guide me forward. When I heard Him say you were the one He had chosen for me, I knew He approved of how I had turned my life around and He knew that I was ready."

Pat did not respond, just looked at him and wondered what else he would come up with to convince her. She could feel herself beginning to soften. He could probably sense it too.

Robert took both of her hands as he continued. "I understand your hesitation. Here I am bum rushing you. If I were in your place, I would want to run far and fast too. But I promise that I have no motive or agenda except to be with you, love you, and build a life with you. And you will never have to compete. I know what's out there and I have no curiosities to satisfy or lust to fulfill except with only one woman: my wife, the one I'm committed to until death do us part."

Pat's voice was trembling. "I want to be loved Robert. Don't get me wrong. My parents loved hard. Each other. Me. Family and friends. I want to be adored and treasured like my mom. And I have a lot of love to give. I want to give it in a 'til death do us part' marriage like they had. I just don't think I'm ready right now. I need to be sure that I can be enough for the next man I marry so that he won't cheat on me. I wasn't enough for my first husband."

Robert pushed back at her. "Did you ever think that you were more than enough and maybe he just wasn't good enough for you? If you are successful at writing about romance, I can't imagine that you wouldn't give all your love in real life. I don't want him to stop you from moving on because he didn't appreciate you. And I definitely don't want him to interfere with what we could have."

Pat was silent, thinking that she did finally come to that conclusion but it had taken so long for the hurt to go away that she was still hesitant to try again.

"Okay Pat. Answer this for me: what do you think it will take for you to get ready, to feel that you are enough for me?" he asked.

She responded slowly, thinking as she spoke. "Time I guess. Time to continue to heal. Time to get to know you. Enough time together to believe that I will be enough for you. So how about this: let's date for a year and if we both are ready at that time we will get married on your next birthday. How does that sound? Can we do that?"

"That's an option" he acknowledged, "but not a viable one for me. I don't like long distance relationships and definitely don't want to just see you once or twice a month. And if I can be real honest with you, I really like being around you and want to be with you every day and sleep with you every night and make love to you often as a part of how I love you, in addition to providing for you and protecting you. And until we are married I intend to be celibate.

"Besides, the real question is will you take a chance with me, to work with me toward what both of our parents had? If the answer to that is yes, then why can't we start now? We are both adults who have been through enough to know what we want."

Again, Pat didn't answer so he continued pressing for her to see his point of view.

"You believe in God right?"

"Of course."

"Do you believe that He speaks to us, that He spoke to me?"

"Yes."

"Then trust me as I trust God. I know without a shadow of a doubt that I heard God's voice say that you were the one He chose for me. That's not a regular occurrence in my life. In fact, I have in times past prayed to hear His voice for different things and heard nothing, so when I hear it, I know I must believe and pay attention to what He is saying to me. Maybe He is saying that my role in your life is to help you heal with all the love I have to give you."

Pat paused to think about that for a moment. Truth be told, God had said that Robert was the answer to her prayers. But who ever heard of something this bizarre — getting *married* on the first night you meet someone? That's what you see in the movies, not in real life, and especially not in Black life. For most Black women, there are too many things they need to get confirmation on to be so impulsive, like his history with women and baby mama status, does he have a criminal record, see where he lives, find out about his credit. She knew very little about him.

"Ok Pat, think about this and be honest: when we met in that restaurant something very unusual and very special happened. When we looked at each other eye to eye we were attracted and immediately connected to one another. And I don't mean in the 'she's pretty and he's handsome so let's sleep together' kind of way. I mean in the 'mind, heart, soul, kindred spirts, we are one, I know this is love' kind of way. I felt it. Did you not feel that too? Be honest. I saw you trying to deny the feelings, acting very cool and trying to pull your hand away. I think you were surprised like I was, but the feelings were real. Right?"

She paused again before answering. If she said no she would be lying and she's not a liar. Those heat waves were very real. Finally she nodded her head yes.

"So let's do this. Let's follow our hearts. Take this leap of faith with me Patricia Harris. In fact, to show good faith, until you are ready, I want the ceremony to happen tonight, and I will sign the marriage license, but we will wait for you to sign it. Legally Tommy has ninety days to file the signed certificate with the county so you have time to decide. There will be no sex, and to be especially clear," he insisted, "I mean NONE - no French kiss, not oral sex, nothing. We will just spend time together to get to know each other. If you never sign it, then we were never married. But once you sign it, it is official and we will commence our married life from that day forward. And we will celebrate our anniversaries on my birthday. Okay?"

Pat was terrified. She had been alone for a while and

needed someone to love her. She was already feeling like a part of the McKnight family and she really, really missed having one of her own.

'Speak to my heart Lord. And be loud and clear. What should I do?' was her prayer and plea. The silence was deafening. Did silence mean consent she wondered?

Robert watched her and could see that his request was a challenge for Pat. Her face got a pensive look as she thought so he told her he would give her space to think, he would be back in a few minutes. He went to his room to pray that God would guide her thoughts and speak to her heart so that she was as convicted as he was that this was the answer to prayers for both of them.

CHAPTER SEVEN

Pat thought about her mom and dad, Paula and Patrick. The story they always told is that they met when he was a junior and she was a freshman in high school, the first day of the school year. They both knew instantly that they were in love and destined to be together for the rest of their lives.

Patrick was a star on the basketball team and had many girls after him. He had fun hanging out with them but no 'girlfriend.' Paula had very little personal experience with boys, mostly crushes on neighborhood boys and a couple of group dates. But she had sisters and all they talked about was boys—how they acted, how they should treat you, what to say no to, how to know when he is 'the one.' And they had a very progressive mother who was happy to weigh in on the conversations when they let her. They had taken all the polls and read all the articles in teen and women's magazines to validate their opinions.

When Paula and Patrick met she knew he was 'the one' based on all the criteria on the various checklists. He trusted his heart and knew she was the one so neither of them ever dated other people. Once he graduated from high school he looked for work that would enable him to take care of her when they began their lives together.

They were married as soon as Paula graduated and Pat was born two years later. They named her Patricia, believing it was a good combination of their names, another way they wanted to reflect their eternal love.

Patrick died at age fifty. The doctor said it was a heart condition called hypertrophic cardiomyopathy, a condition where the heart muscles become abnormally thick and it's hard to pump blood. It had never revealed itself before and he always made his annual doctor appointments. Talk about gone too soon.

Paula never fully recovered from losing her beloved husband. She was functional enough to work, but was eating poorly, losing weight, and began drinking excessively. She never dated another man. She lived with a depression that never seemed to end. When Pat asked her mother why she had loved her husband so hard, she was given the advice that she needed today to help her decide what to do.

Paula had a smile on her face as she counseled her daughter. "You will meet all kinds of men in your dating life: kind men, mean men, smart men. Some will be serious, others fun and even funny, cute or even really handsome. Some may not be classically handsome but they will be sexy and attractive to you. Nice guys, bad boys, players.

"They will sweet talk you, wine and dine you, and make you feel good. One day I hope you will fall in love and get married to one of the great ones that you love and who demonstrates that he really loves you.

"But if you are really lucky, as I was, I hope you will meet the man who makes you feel the way your dad made me feel the day we met and throughout our marriage. You will know that your heart and soul have been satisfied and your life is already complete. Other men will not compare or be able to offer what he does to make you happy. Then you will know why it is hard for me to date and settle for less. I don't need another man. I've had it all."

"How will I know him?' Pat asked.

"Easy" Paula responded. "He will bring a heat unlike anything you have ever felt in your life. You will feel it physically, his warmth radiating all over you very intensely. And he will be feeling the heat from you the same way. It will happen suddenly, so you won't see it coming and you will not be able to stop it.

"He will look at you and really see you for who you are and you will feel the unconditional love he has for you. It will take your breath away. He will be quick and decisive and stalk you like a Panther surrounding his prey, never letting you out of his sight until you surrender to his love.

"Keep in mind that the same passion can be equally strong in the tough times. Every couple goes through something. But the Panther Heat reminds you of why you're together and will get you through."

"Sounds scary," Pat responded with a frown on her face.

"Yes," Paula said, "It is, but in the best kind of way.

If you ever get that feeling, grab hold to it and enjoy the ride. It is the greatest feeling you will ever know. Not everybody gets to experience it, but the best relationships and marriages do."

Pat thought about her first marriage. She met Eric at the law firm where they were both working while she was in graduate school. She was in the communications department, providing quality control for clarity, punctuation, and grammar before documents were submitted to court. He had been a criminal attorney for about three years already, but recognized it was time to get serious and become a family man if he wanted to be a partner and be successful. Tall and slender with deep black eyes, he was smart, nice looking, charismatic and fun. He pursued her for months before she would go out with him. She was busy with school and work and didn't have much time. Eventually she said yes. They dated over a year and Pat grew to love him. They were well suited: both ambitious, high achievers, and fun. When he surprised her by proposing, she said yes! She was excited. This was her happily ever after and she couldn't wait to have the kind of loving marriage her parents had.

Things were very nice for a good little while. He was attentive. She worked to please him, to be the wife he said he wanted, from her appearance to cooking to sex. She thought they were happy for a little over two years though it was never with the heat that her mom described.

But Robert...Robert was accomplished in his career and not looking for anyone to validate him or make him appealing to the partners like Eric when he asked her to marry him. Robert was fun, and very attentive even though he could have his pick of women to give him attention. He seemed settled in his life but ready to get married and create a family. And the chemistry was hard to avoid. He was like a walking sex magnet, bringing the heat her mother described. It was scary, but very compelling at the same time. Hard to walk away from. And Paula said to grab hold and enjoy the ride.

With Robert, she could feel that cascading warm sensation, the Panther Heat. It was between them everywhere they were tonight: in the restaurant, in the car despite the fact that he had irritated her, in the kitchen, and even now. It was intense. They were connected in a way she had never felt before, with anyone.

Robert came back to the family room after about fifteen minutes. He sat on the sofa and leaned back, pulling Pat into his arms so that her head rested on his chest and just held her until she was ready to respond. His hugs felt warm and comforting. Soothing even. She needed them. She needed him. He had the Panther Heat.

Finally, Pat nodded yes. Robert hugged her and whispered in her ear, "I've got you. Trust me."

Robert was excited and started calling for Tommy and Shelly even before he got to their bedroom door. He shouted for them to come out, they had a wedding to perform. When Shelly opened the door, she was laughing and told Tommy to pay her $20 for winning the bet.

Tommy said he thought Pat was very nice and good for Robert, but he bet that she would say no. He shared with a laugh, "Chicago women are not likely to move quickly, especially into a marriage. They are often hard to convince to do something this life-changing."

Shelly said she bet on her brother because he knew how to get whatever he really wanted.

Robert kissed Shelly on the cheek and patted Tommy on the back laughing and saying, "Man, you don't know that about me yet? I want this woman and she was not leaving here or leaving me until she said yes."

Tommy laughed and gave Shelly the money as he went to his study for the paperwork and a Bible. Shelly told her brother she was happy that he had finally found the right woman. She hugged Pat and said she had always wanted a sister, especially now. With Tommy, TJ, and Bobby, she sometimes felt overwhelmed by the testosterone in her life.

TJ came down from his room to say goodnight and asked why Ms. Pat was crying. Robert explained to him, "I've asked Ms. Pat to marry me and officially join the family tonight, right now, and she is nervous and scared."

TJ had never seen his uncle smile so much around a woman so he could tell his Uncle Bobby was happy. Plus TJ liked her too so he was very happy to hear that she was going to marry into the family. He wrapped his arms around her and said, "Don't cry Ms. Pat. We already love you. May I call you Aunt Pat now?" Pat nodded yes through her tears. She was feeling overwhelmed but excited too.

Robert asked TJ to be his best man and Pat asked

Shelly to stand with her as her new sister. It was a perfect circle of love as Tommy committed them to God as a couple and a family, and united Robert to Pat and Pat to Robert so that they would learn to love and grow and journey through life together forever as one. Robert pulled Pat into his arms and kissed her on her forehead, her nose, and both cheeks, then gently pressed his lips to hers for just a second to affirm their marriage.

When the ceremony was over, Robert signed the certificate and there were hugs all around. He walked Pat over to the sofa and sat with her to confirm that she was okay and thank her for putting her trust in him. "I know you are scared. Just know that I'm not. This feels so good and so right that I'm excited and ready. I hope you will soon be as well." She was quiet and watchful, smiling as he talked. She liked his confidence and was glad he had enough for both of them. He asked her to wait while he spoke with TJ about the activities for their day together on Saturday. Pat could tell at the restaurant that there was a special bond between the two of them and thought that Robert was likely a good man after all. At the same time, she knew a male/female relationship would be different so she would not throw caution completely to the wind.

Shelly could see Pat was tired and offered that she should rest in Robert's Room. She remarked that he could sometimes be a while with TJ if they played a video game or two. Shelly then asked Pat how she was doing. She replied honestly, "I don't know." Pat told Shelly what her mother had said and that Robert was making her feel the way she described so she was fearful but hopeful.

Shelly shared with Pat, "Robert has always been very focused and decisive, even as a kid. He knew what he wanted and accepted no substitutes, not in clothes or food or toys or friends.

"He was easy to love as a brother because we talked about everything. He told me what he liked and didn't like and what he wanted and never wavered. I never had to guess about what was going on with him. And he was supportive and protective, especially after our folks died."

She assured Pat that Robert was one of the good guys and she was looking forward to seeing their relationship develop. "He loves hard and will almost ruthlessly protect what is his and who he loves. But he is also sensitive. He might back away if he feels like he's been wronged and definitely if you say you don't want him."

"Wow. Really? Should I be afraid?" Pat was a little concerned.

"No. There is no better man, other than my own husband." Shelly smiled.

Pat thought about her mother again and said, "Well it sounds scary, the way my mom said it would be. I guess I will just have to hang on and see what happens."

By the time Robert came back downstairs Shelly and Tommy had retired to bed and he found Pat had dozed off on top of the covers in the bed in his room. It had been a long day and she had not planned to be out so late. Nor had she expected such an evening of celebration and the stress of a wedding ceremony.

He did not wake her up. Instead, he watched her for

a few minutes and thanked God for the way things worked out. Then he changed his shirt and pants for a t-shirt and pajama bottoms, got a blanket out of the closet and got in on the other side of the bed. He moved close to Pat so that her back and head rested on his chest and their bodies were close together, stretched out side by side, his arm around her. Making sure the blanket covered them both, he was settling in for a good night's sleep when he heard a soft moan escape Pat's lips and she woke up. She could hear him say under his breath "Yes, it feels good to me too. Sweet dreams my wife, my love." She snuggled closer to him. They both slept hard, like they could finally relax from the challenges of single life, dating, and living alone.

CHAPTER EIGHT

When Pat woke up, she heard Robert say, "Good morning Mrs. McKnight." She had not moved or even opened her eyes so it was odd he could sense that she was awake, especially when her back was to him. She stretched and yawned, then rolled over to look at him and take in her surroundings. "Yes, we did that, huh? Wedding ceremony." She looked like she was thinking over whether this was a good thing or not, then smiled and responded softly with "Good morning husband." His eyes lit up. He really wanted to kiss her but knew better. That was not part of the deal.

She sat up, listening for house sounds and looking for a clock or her cell phone. "It's quiet. What time is it? Where's the rest of the family?"

Robert checked the time on his cell phone then responded. "It's eight o'clock. They are gone to work and school. We are here alone. Are you hungry? May I fix breakfast for you? Or would you rather go out?" He was eager to please for their first morning together.

Pat was surprised when she realized how comfortable and safe she felt, like she was at home even in Shelly and Tommy's house. She wanted to enjoy the morning but get home soon to shower and change. First, she wanted to have some fun with Robert. "You cook? Can I expect this every morning? What's on the menu?"

He responded quickly. "Yes, I cook. Not every day. I have to work. Mostly weekends. Anything you want. As you know, Shelly keeps a fully stocked kitchen. Or we can go out." He was relishing the quiet and getting a chance to talk with her alone. "Are you a coffee drinker? Or tea in the morning? Or just juice? Water?" There's so much to get to know. I must admit that I am excited."

Pat smiled as she responded. "I can see that. Me too. Let's start slow. Not a coffee drinker. Maybe water, but first I want to freshen up. I'll meet you in the kitchen in ten minutes. I'll have whatever you're having."

He cooked the traditional southern breakfast of bacon, fried eggs, grits, and toast and it was ready by the time she walked into the kitchen. "It smells good in here!" She was happy and you could hear it in her voice. "And you look like you know your way around a kitchen. What's your favorite thing to cook? Do you have a specialty?"

He confessed. "I'm real basic in the kitchen. Breakfast I'm ok, and sandwiches, but some of the other stuff, not so much. I eat out a lot. Can you cook?"

"I can cook some things. I'm good with recipes and I like to experiment. How would you feel about us cooking together? Combine skills and create great meals?" She offered a compromise because she did not want to be the designated cook for life. He nodded yes to that. They said grace and talked about the activities for the day.

"I need to go home and shower and change before we do anything. What did you have in mind after that?" She was open to whatever he wanted to do. She didn't have to work again until Monday.

"We have to get the marriage license first," Robert reminded her. "Then maybe we can go to the Galleria Shopping Mall and hang out for a little while. I want to spend the rest of the week-end with you. May I stay at your place? We need to keep getting to know each other."

She said yes, and prepared to head home. Robert would follow in about an hour or so after cleaning the kitchen and getting dressed.

On her way home was the first time she had to fully assess the events of the past twenty-four hours without interruption or pressure. She had enjoyed meeting Robert and his family and admitted that she was crazy to say yes to his proposal. Had she truly lost her mind? Loneliness can make you do very foolish things.

But Pat knew she had to take the chance. Her mom's words kept replaying in her head. She saw how her mom and dad loved one another and lived for each other and how strong their bond remained even in death. If she could get what they had, or even come close, it was worth a shot. Even though he wasn't there, Pat could feel Robert's presence, remembering how he watched her with such intensity, and feeling that he meant what he said.

Robert came at noon for their first 'date.' He dropped his bag in the entry hall and took a slow walk through her two-bedroom apartment. Her style was contemporary with vibrant colors in the print sofa and burgundy chairs. He noticed that her TV stand, dressers and lamps were black, commenting that black was his favorite color in home furnishings too. Books and artwork caught his attention and he asked about the number of birds in her art and accessories. Pat explained, "The art belonged to my Mom and birds were her favorite so I kept them all." Her office was sparse but comfortable: a laptop and printer on a small desk, a desk chair and a few books.

Her vision board was on the front of the refrigerator, pictures and notes of all her hopes and dreams. "Who is this man?" Robert asked quietly about the picture of a model she had found on the internet. "I don't know him," she responded. "He is a placeholder until God sends the right man for me." He took the magnets off and laid the picture on the counter. "I'll let you handle getting rid of that," he whispered in her ear.

He saw the floor plan of a house and looked at her to explain.

"It's my idea of a dream house. One level. Every bedroom has its own bathroom plus there is a powder room. Big enough for a family but cozy at the same time."

"Okay, okay" Robert said in a very affirmative tone, slowly nodding his head. Then he asked about the pictures of the car. "Why a Porsche? What is so special about it?"

She playfully acted as if she was amazed he didn't get

it right away and pointed out, "It's not just any Porsche, but a Porsche *Panamera*. I can't really explain much more than the fact that it looks sleek, sexy, and powerful to me." Like you, she said to herself.

"I test drove one and loved the feel of it and the features, and I'm always drawn to them when I see them on the street. If there is one within a two block radius I can feel it, then I wait and watch for it to roll by."

He could see from her expression that she got very excited just talking about it. Chuckling, he asked, "So you're sure that's what you want?" She nodded yes and he said, "Okay. We will work on that."

He made himself comfortable, leaning back in a living room chair while they talked. She liked that. This apartment, her haven from the world, felt good with this man in it.

Their first stop was to City Hall to get the marriage license. Next, he found a place for them to take blood tests so that they could confirm each other to be 'clean.' Then on to the Galleria to have lunch and look at rings. "Not to buy today," he clarified. "I do not want to put that pressure on you, but it will give me an idea of what you like, what my ring could look like, and our ring sizes."

Throughout the day he held her hand. Sometimes he would put his hand playfully on her neck and rub it then pull her close to him. Sometimes his arm was around her waist. Always touching her. The chemistry was really good between them. It felt new and fresh and exciting. But she wondered if he was the clingy, jealous type and needed to always show others that she belonged to him. She decided to enjoy the moments and let his personality and intentions unfold without her second-guessing his every move.

They sat for a while to watch the shoppers and decide their next stop, sitting side by side on the bench in the middle of the mall, holding hands. She commented on the fact that he liked to hold hands. He asked, "Are you uncomfortable?" and prepared to withdraw his hand.

"Not uncomfortable, just curious," she replied, not letting him pull his hand away.

He proceeded to give her a lesson on the importance and value of touching to the human body and spirit. "Did you know that babies need to be held regularly so they don't grow up with mental or emotional issues from sensory deprivation? That's why they have people work or volunteer in hospitals who do nothing but hold and talk to the babies who don't have families or who need extra stimulation.

"And did you know that hands have the most nerve endings in the body? Holding hands helps to activate cortisol, which reduces stress and blood pressure; and it increases oxytocin, which generates the feelings of connection and communication between people. I think it's working. I already feel connected to you."

His face and voice tone were so serious Pat didn't know what to say except, "Okay."

Then he laughed and blushed like a little kid saying, "The truth is I just like being with you and being close to you. You are very sexy to me, and your hands are soft and a perfect fit in mine. And you smell so good you are like a magnet. I just want to be close to you all the time. This is very unusual for me. I am not usually the touchy, feely type. Most women find me cold, standoff-ish. If you are uncomfortable or I am embarrassing you, just say so. It's ok. I will respect that. But hey, since we're not having sex, can a brother have something to hold on to?"

They both laughed at that and Pat felt some relief that he sounded 'normal.' For the rest of the day he would hold her hand then look at her as if asking permission. It became their private joke so she relaxed and made sure she was always near him every time he reached for her. She loved that he wanted to hold hands and be close. That was her love language too.

They had a fun leisurely afternoon at the mall, found rings they both loved and did some window shopping to get an idea of each others style and preferences in clothes and shoes and accessories. It was getting late so they ordered pizza to be delivered for dinner and headed back to Pat's apartment. Saturday was going to be a busy day for Robert and Pat wanted to use the time to think about the book she wanted to start writing in the next week or two. She also wanted to think about the possibilities with Robert since she still felt the heat after being together all day.

When it was time for bed, Pat wasn't sure what to do. She usually wore a tank top or tee shirt with pajama pants. With this man, though, she wondered if she should dress up a little, maybe put on a cute gown? With their no sex commitment, she shouldn't tease right?

Robert knocked on the bathroom door to ask if she was okay and what was taking so long. When Pat explained her dilemma, he laughed and said "your usual is fine with me. We are going to sleep, but thanks for being considerate."

Sleeping in bed with him at Shelly and Tommy's was nice. She was nestled in his arms and felt covered and secure. This time though, in the middle of her queen-sized bed, he wrapped his whole body around her. It felt like a warm cocoon. He said "Sweet dreams my wife, my love."

He was a true gentleman. Pat admired his restraint. She slept like a baby, thinking that those long nights of insomnia might finally be over.

The next morning he again knew she was awake before she opened her eyes and greeted her with, "Good morning Sunshine." Her reply, "Good morning husband," put a smile on his face and also helped her get used to the idea that she was committed to working on their marriage.

She headed to the bathroom to get dressed. When she came back into the room, he was lounging in bed and told her that he thought she looked sexy trying not to be sexy, and he was very happy simply holding her soft curvy body. Pat took the opportunity to sit on the bed with him and ask why he found it necessary to be so explicit in defining 'no sex.' He hesitated before responding.

"I was always particular about the women I slept with and what I did with them. I know women sleep around like men sometimes so I never wanted to be too expressive outside of a committed relationship. I just like to be clear. I want this relationship to be about us, not how good the sex is, as I expect it will be, and how that might cloud our judgement on whether we should be together."

"Okay," was all Pat could say. She was intrigued. He was so attractive to her and she knew she was attractive to him, and since neither of them were virgins waiting seemed unnecessary. At the same time, she liked that sex was taken out of the equation and they could focus on being together and getting to know each other. Imagining the sex when they did finally consummate their marriage made her very excited. And warm and tingly all over her body.

This time it was Pat's turn to cook breakfast while Robert got dressed. She kept it simple with oatmeal, toast and sausage because Robert said TJ had found a food truck festival and he figured they would eat their way through the day. Before he left to hang out with TJ, Robert asked Pat to go home to Dallas with him on Sunday and stay until he came back for his next visit to Houston.

She protested. "I have a job. People are counting on me. I can come up on the week-end."

He was adamant. "They need to get used to being without you. I will give you money to make up for not getting a paycheck. Besides, I've waited a long time for you and I want to be with you. And not just week-ends." He kept talking. "If this is going to work we need to be together. Remember our vows: from this day forward…?"

She couldn't think of an argument to any of that and said okay.

While Robert was out with TJ, Pat called her supervisor, Maggie, at the bookstore, explaining that she needed a leave of absence immediately and could not give her a return date. She told her it was personal and because Maggie respected Pat and her work ethic, she didn't pry, saying okay, just keep her posted on when she might be coming back. It helped that Pat had been there over three years and had been a good employee, always showing up on time, staying over when asked, or being a last minute fill-in. Maggie knew it had to be serious for Pat to call with such a last minute request and no idea about a return date.

Pat had a lot of clothes and shoes so it took a couple of hours to pack, not knowing what they would be doing in Dallas and how much she would need. In typical fashion, she packed too much, but she was prepared for all possible events.

Robert met Pat's Houston family at their regular Sunday brunch. Aunt Ginny (Virginia) and Uncle Roy had two adult children, Gina (Regina), and Roy Jr., who was married to Wanda and together they had a year old baby boy. There were about ten family members who got together consistently every week at their house, including some other relatives and friends who were like family.

Pat didn't date much after her marriage and definitely didn't bring any of them around the family since they usually didn't last long. Her aunt and uncle were totally shocked when she announced that this was the guy she was with the night she sent the text, and they had a wedding ceremony, and she was going to Dallas with him for an extended stay. They knew about her first marriage so they were hesitant to give their blessings until they knew what this speedy relationship was about.

Robert was quiet at first, getting to know who was who and how they were all related.

Uncle Roy took them out to the patio to let Robert know how important Pat was to him and his wife and they were concerned, needing to understand this impulsive decision to get married without knowing one another. "We love Pat like a daughter and we know she's grown and can make her own decisions. But we need to feel comfortable about you, especially since you are taking her out of town, away from us. Thankfully, her aunts and some cousins are in the Dallas-Ft. Worth area so we will still have family to watch out for her. But why so fast son?"

Robert looked at Uncle Roy and held Pat's hand as he spoke. "I can understand your concerns and want to assure you and your wife that I will not harm her. Honesty, integrity, good relationships, whether they are family or not, are important to me. My intentions are honorable which is why I wanted marriage and not just dating.

"I turned forty on Thursday, and for the last fifteen or so years I have been focused on my career. It's only been lately that I decided I needed a wife and family life. I guess that's why Pat appeared. I'm ready. Pat and I already agree that we want a relationship like our parents had: loyal, loving, fun."

"Why do you think Patricia is the one when you don't even know her?" Uncle Roy was perplexed.

Robert paused before answering that one. Then he said, "I've been a pretty good judge of character all of my life. When she had dinner with me and my family the first night I met her, she was confident, genuinely friendly, asked interesting questions, and wasn't 'thirsty' for a man if you know what I mean. And obviously she's beautiful. She reminded me of my mother. I sincerely believe she is the one for me and a good fit in my family."

"What happens when you get to know her and it doesn't work out?" Uncle Roy knew that Pat was no pushover and had seen her feisty side through the years as she played and fought with her cousins.

"I'm sure we'll work out. Might have a few bumps in the road, but we will get to know each other as we work them out. If by some chance we don't stay together, I will make sure she's ok and wish her well. I would be hurt, but I will want her to be happy."

Robert was sincere and forthright with his answers. He knew how important Uncle Roy was to Pat and her family as the elder statesman. And he could feel the love Uncle Roy had for Pat's dad and that he took his responsibility seriously to make sure she was okay, doing the right thing. He was protecting Pat.

How he handled her uncle's concerns also gave Pat more insight into Roberts's character.

When Uncle Roy went back into the house, Pat

thanked Robert for the way he spoke and the way he made her feel more confident in her decision. With stomachs growling, they rejoined the family for brunch.

The food was good and Robert ate heartily, played dominoes, then joined in the fight over Chicago Bulls versus Houston Rockets and Dallas Mavericks as they all were playing in the finals. It got loud, especially as they argued over who was the 'GOAT' (greatest of all time) between Michael Jordan and LeBron James, but all in fun. Robert fit right in.

Uncle Roy and Aunt Ginny pulled her aside after the game and said they liked him so far. Aunt Ginny explained, "He has good manners and seems genuine and fun. We can tell he likes you by the way he keeps looking at you, like your father used to look at your mom, making sure she was close by and that she was okay and having a good time. Robert looks at you like that." This was a pleasant surprise to Pat since she had been so busy laughing and talking with her cousins she had not noticed. Everyone wished them well as they were leaving for Dallas.

CHAPTER NINE

Robert was tired from driving to Houston and the activities over the week-end so Pat volunteered to drive. He was happy to let her so he could relax and sleep.

Pat spent time thinking about how quickly things had changed in her life in just four days. First, the two book deal. Aside from the excitement of it all, she was grateful. It was validation that she had talent and she was being noticed. So many great Black writers never got recognition with traditional publishers.

Then on the same Thursday evening, she met a charming, handsome, persistent Black man who seemed to have all the characteristics she had been wanting plus a nice family who welcomed her with open arms. So she said yes to marrying him and agreed to the ceremony the same night! She thought there must have been something hypnotic in his eyes or cologne to make her respond to him like that. She had never been so easily persuaded.

As she continued to reflect, she had to admit that Friday had been a fun day with Robert. Relaxing, casual, sensual. He was very focused on her and made sure she understood that this force of attraction pulling them together was not a one-time fling. So when he asked her to go home to Dallas with him on Saturday, she knew it was the next logical step, her weak protests aside. They needed to explore the possibilities together. This was taking 'no risk no reward' to a whole new level. Thankfully, when he met her family at brunch today they had seen some of what she saw so their approval gave her an added measure of confidence. Now she was ready for the adventure of Robert McKnight. Still, she prayed to God as she drove to keep speaking to her heart and affirming that this was right and Robert was really the man for her. Then she thought about the Panther Heat. Could this actually be the love of her life?

About half way to Dallas Robert woke up but didn't open his eyes. He startled Pat when he started talking. "You are a good driver Pat. Do you like to drive?"

"I do." She explained, "My grandfather taught me when I was eleven and I've been driving ever since. Before I got my license my parents let me drive to school by myself on really cold days, and sometimes my mom let me drive us to church for Sunday service. My parents liked to drive too. Our vacations were mostly car trips so we could spend time together, enjoy the landscape of the country, and experience different cities. How about you?"

She stole a peek at him. He finally opened his eyes as he responded.

"Yes, I like to drive. My dad taught me and bought me a car when I turned sixteen. I started working right away to put gas in it and pay for the oil changes and other maintenance."

Then he suggested, "Since we both like to drive, maybe we could take some driving trips this summer? I would love to drive through parts of the south that I've never visited, or places I passed through for business but didn't have a chance to stay and explore the area."

She liked that he was already planning things for them. "Yes, let's do that. It would be fun."

Robert then asked Pat to tell him more about herself. "Talking with Uncle Roy made me realize that I don't know enough about you. In the restaurant you talked about your writing and gave a snap shot version of you. You have my undivided attention for this last two hundred miles. Fill in some details please."

Pat was happy to share. "The Harris family was pretty cool. My mom and dad fell in love the first day she went to high school. He was a junior, and they immediately decided they only wanted to be with each other for the rest of their lives. My dad started his own service business right out of high school so he could be ready to take care of my mom when she graduated. He was good with his hands, building and fixing things around the house and fixing cars. He was an electrician by trade. He used all of those talents and was very successful. My mom started working right out of high school and went to junior college, getting her associates degree. She rose through the ranks of city government to become Vice President, Chief Information Officer for two Mayors. I was born after they had been married two years.

Robert listened attentively then commented, "It's interesting that your parents story is not that different from mine, taking a chance on love right away even though they waited to actually get married. My folks always said they knew when they met but waited until he was able to make enough money to take care of them before getting married."

Pat acknowledged the similarities too. "What are the odds, huh?"

She continued to tell her story. "Our home was happy and fun and always full of family— aunts and uncles and cousins in and out, some even staying for a while when they got on my aunt's nerves. I have a few close friends in Chicago and Houston who are like family to me, and with all my cousins, I am surrounded by good people who I know always have my back.

"It was a great life until my dad died. My mom died of a stroke brought on by uncontrolled high blood pressure, in my mind more like uncontrolled grief, never recovering from my dad's death." She paused to think about her folks. There was no sadness, just proud reflections.

"I told you about my imagination and vivid dreams, even as a child. No scenario was too farfetched for me to make up a skit and act out with my dolls or my cousins. I was everything from a diva entertainer/actor to a scary killer and wrote the dialogue for everyone. I would have a dream then wake up and write notes. Some dreams were typical, about family, or travel, or visions of what to do with my life. Sometimes they were episodes from the news or television shows.

"As I grew older I dreamed a lot of romance with hot, sexy men, probably filling a void in my life before I got married. One time I dreamed that I was a man having an orgasm. It gave me clear insight into why men were so interested in having sex. It was a powerful experience, much more intense than female orgasms. Whenever I dreamed of being pregnant or having a baby, three people would soon die in real life. When I dreamed of death, somebody close to me was pregnant. It never failed."

He was intrigued by her mind and imagination and couldn't wait to read some of her writing. The more he learned about her the happier he was with his decision to press her to get married right away.

Pat continued. "While in grad school to get my masters in Journalism, I worked summers as a correspondence manager for a law firm. I created and updated form letters and documents to clients and edited and proofread briefs for court for content and context, and spelling, grammatical and punctuation errors. After graduation, I taught night classes at one of the local junior colleges in addition to working full-time for the law firm. I like helping others learn.

"Once my marriage ended I decided to use my mom's insurance money and proceeds from the sale of the family home to follow my passion and write for a living. I often turned the dreams and my theories on relationships into topics for articles that got me paid, including the couple of romance novellas. For steady income I work in bookstores."

"Well now you can think about just focusing on your writing. Would you like that or do you prefer working?"

Robert knew she didn't need to work for the money but he admired her desire to be active and engaged with others. He would support whatever she decided.

Pat hesitated before responding. "I don't know. It's a lot to think about and there is so much for us to get through first in getting to know each other. Let's see what happens."

CHAPTER TEN

Robert lived in a gated community in Highland Park, one of the nicer suburbs of Dallas. His house was beautiful, but he and Shelly had totally different styles. Surprisingly, it was similar to the floor plan Pat had on her vision board: a contemporary brick ranch, almost 4,000 square feet, family room, four bedrooms, four and a half baths, an office, and media room. Open concept. Enough space for two and they wouldn't get lost from one another, yet large enough for a family and to entertain. The kitchen was the focal point of the home, and the island was huge. Little did she know, the kitchen would turn out to be a focal point of their lives too as they got to know each other.

There was hardly any furniture in the house: a large black sectional sofa and 70" flat screen in the family room; a brand new king-sized mattress in the master along with an old clock radio on the floor next to it, a keepsake from his parents' house that he used to wake him up at six every morning; and bar height chairs at the kitchen counter. Robert had not been cooking so he mostly had paper plates and plastic forks and knives for his takeout food in the kitchen. His dishes, cutlery, cooking utensils, and pots and pans were still packed away, sitting in the pantry.

All the other rooms were empty.

"Why this house? And is this your idea of minimalist living?" Pat was curious.

He explained, "This was part of my renewal. When I knew it was time to find a wife, I decided to move out of what Shelly called my bachelor pad and buy a house, a fresh start. I like contemporary houses, clean lines, open spaces. I liked that each bedroom has its own bathroom. Like the floor plan on your vision board.

"So I'm renting my bachelor pad condo fully furnished, and I bought new pieces but only what was absolutely necessary for me. I figured my wife would want to decorate. In the meantime, I needed something to sit on and a bed to sleep in."

He asked Pat if she liked the house and promised that no other woman had visited there except his sister. "This house is yours. For us. If you don't like this one, we could find another more to your liking."

She didn't say anything to him immediately, but as they walked through each room Pat knew exactly where her furniture and pictures and accessories would go. She was happy. She could see making this their home and told him so saying, "I like it a lot Robert. We have similar tastes. With a little more furniture it could be a cozy home."

Robert was quick to say that her furniture would help make it cozy so as soon as she was ready, they could pack her up and get it to Dallas. He shrugged his shoulders and commented, "I'm just saying…"

Pat rolled her eyes and instead of responding to his comment, asked him if she could have one of the three extra bedrooms just for her – her clothes and toiletries and "office." She wanted privacy and to preserve some of herself to reveal to him later.

He thought it was odd and unnecessary since the master bedroom and bathroom were huge and there already was an office she could use but he said ok. "It's your house to use any way you choose, just be in bed with me at night," he said with a wink and a sexy smile.

He didn't have to worry about that, Pat thought. She always wanted to be in bed with him and wrapped in his arms. Now that she was committed to trying to see if they could be a couple, she was also getting very curious about making love with him, imagining how attentive he would be to her needs, and if her limited experience would be enough for him.

He gave her the code to the house and key fobs to both cars, 'house money' for groceries and gas and whatever else was needed. Then he asked how much her monthly bills were.

Pat was surprised and asked why he needed to know that.

"I promised to make up for the money you lose by not working. I want to cover your monthly expenses so you won't have to think about that while you are here."

She told him and was shocked when he told her he was sending three months worth of expense money through her cash app.

"Why so much?" Pat was uncomfortable. She had never had a man take care of her like that. She even paid some of the household bills when she was married.

"You have ninety days to sign the certificate. I want you to take all the time you need to decide and not get hung up on getting back to work."

She was overwhelmed and tears welled up in her eyes. When he saw them, he pulled her into his arms and whispered, "I hope those are happy tears." He kissed her forehead and both eyes before tears could fall.

She nodded yes so he held her longer, telling her "I want to make you happy but not to make you cry." Then he asked "What else can I do to make you happy Patricia Harris McKnight? And hey, do you have a middle name? Will you hyphenate your name or just be Patricia McKnight?"

Pat responded quietly, speaking into his chest, "My middle name is Elaine, and I don't believe in hyphenated names."

He pulled her closer and said "Good. I was hoping you would say that. And what else can I do to make you happy Patricia Elaine?" Holding her close made him realize that his body was waking up from celibacy so he had to be very careful. He wanted to kiss her in the mouth and make love to her. She could tell too, feeling him growing hard and pressing against her stomach. They slowly broke apart yet he still wanted an answer. He looked at her while waiting for her response.

She thought for a moment then said, "Three things: I want you to give me your best Robert McKnight so I always feel loved and cherished. Always be honest with me. And make sure we connect with each other every day, even when it's not the happiest of our days."

"I can do that" he assured her.

"I hope so Robert. Because these are the things that will keep me believing in us. I don't want to ever doubt you or your love."

CHAPTER ELEVEN

The first hurdle they had was fitting her into his already full life. He works Monday through Friday and goes to the gym on Tuesday and Thursday nights. On the other evenings, he often has meetings for one of the many groups he is involved with: the Dallas Chamber of Commerce, the Urban League and NAACP, the local chapter of the National Association of Accountant's, and an organization whose goal was to end drunk driving known as FAAR – Foundation for Advancing Alcohol Responsibility. He is even active with his homeowners association. On Saturdays every week when he is in town, he and his friends play basketball at the gym. Once or twice a month he goes to the gun range too. The good news was that Friday evenings were open even though he was usually tired, and Sundays were open all day!

His phone rang a lot. He let her know that between family and the different sets of friends and business relationships (college, work, the organizations, the community), everybody seemed to want to talk to him, for information, sharing ideas or the details of their lives, or just to vent. He promised to always make sure she knew to whom he was talking and if they were busy he would tell the caller he would have to call them back.

He wanted her to understand why he had such a busy schedule so he explained. "Part of my job, in fact, the job of all of the partners, is to know as many city officials and local business owners as possible, and to have some presence in the community, to be visible to potential clients as well as keep an eye out for good talent for the company. We want to grow our business and not rely exclusively on government contracts."

Pat decided she should speak up and let him know how she was feeling about all of his activities and where she could fit in. "I'm used to being alone and finding things to do with my time, but I'm not alone now and I'm not in Houston where I have a job, friends, and know where to go and what to do. I don't want to be a nuisance to my family to fill my time, nor do I want to get a job or find writing groups and other organizations to get involved with until I know that I am staying. You leave for work around seven in the morning so waiting for you to come home every night at nine or ten o'clock is not going to work for me."

He compromised by picking one or two organizations to attend their meetings once a month or once a quarter, and the rest he would just support financially and watch for their newsletters and email updates. He would only play ball every other Saturday.

She was happy with his new schedule and gave him a hug to show her appreciation.

"Don't worry," Robert assured her, "I will make sure there is time for you, for us. In fact, I want us to date."

Pat was puzzled. "How is that going to work when we already live together?"

"It will work well I hope." He was smiling as he spoke. "I still need to win your heart and that usually means people date and get to know each other and have special times together, making memories. So will you go out with me Mrs. McKnight? Let me wine and dine you and sweep you off your feet?" Pat of course said yes, excited because she thought that was so romantic.

His goal was, over time, to take her to all the great restaurants in the Dallas-Ft. Worth area. He would get them season tickets to both the Black and White theatres and the Mavericks games, and he wanted them to visit the comedy clubs and go to concerts when their favorite entertainers came to town.

On Monday and Wednesday nights, she was excited to know he would come home at six. She planned to stop work at four or soon after then shower and put on a little makeup and something flirty and always greet him with a smile, a hug, a cold beverage and dinner started. They made plans to cook together on Monday and Wednesday and on the weekends to experiment with how they liked their food seasoned and who could really cook what. Since he was an early riser and good with breakfast and sandwiches, and she liked to try different meat recipes and salad dressings, and they agreed to steamed or sautéed vegetables, they were certain to complement each other nicely and knew they could probably make tasty meals together and have fun in the process.

On Tuesday and Thursday, when he was at the gym,

her plan was that she would work on her book into the evening, then shower and put on her nightclothes, greeting him in the family room or in bed.

On the first day after her arrival in Dallas, the first week of their new life began. Robert went to work and Pat started her own schedule. Robert's gym was close to the house and had all the equipment she used and classes she liked so he changed his membership from individual to family. She unpacked the boxes of kitchen items that were in the pantry, went to the gym after breakfast, then checked email and worked on her first book. She had a storyline in mind but needed to identify the characters, their individual stories as well as the scenario that would bring them together. She also needed to figure out what the obstacles were that they had to face and overcome.

Robert called her after he ate lunch and asked her about her day, told her about his, then asked her out on Friday night. He was surprised at how normal it felt to want to call her in the middle of his day and hear her voice. He had never done that before, always calling women after work, what he called keeping a separation between church (work) and state (women). He had a feeling he would be calling Pat every day about the same time, giving him the boost he needed to tackle his work in the afternoon. He loved her voice. It was sexy and calm and soothing. He promised he would also call on his way home to see if he needed to stop at the store for anything. He knew she could text him. It was another excuse to hear her talk.

The first Monday night when he came home Pat had

R&B music playing and was singing and dancing in the kitchen as she set the table and prepped the food. When Robert walked in through the garage door and saw her, he dropped his keys, cell phone, and jacket on the island and pulled her into the family room so they could dance together. She was surprised and pulled back from him so he challenged her. "Come on now. People from Chicago always think they got a lock on how to dance. What is it called there – Stepping? Show me what you've got Chi-town." He spun her around and she fell right in rhythm with his moves. Their first song together was Chaka Khan's *Ain't Nobody*. When the song ended, Robert clapped his hands to say she was a good dancer and he enjoyed dancing with her. She clapped back to him saying, "Pretty smooth Mr. McKnight."

The first Tuesday evening when he got home from the gym she was in her room, engrossed with sticky notes all over a large board she had brought from her apartment in Houston that was half cork, half whiteboard. It was nailed into the wall next to the card table she was using for a desk. The notes were for reference on her characters and the whiteboard helped her outline the story. She forgot what time it was so she had not showered and prepared for bed as she had planned.

Robert pulled up a chair and asked her to explain her writing process. "I told you I've never met a writer so I'd like to know what you do that results in a book that people will read." He was intrigued by it all and also wanted to let her know he was interested in all of her, especially what he knew was such a big part of her life. She was happy to give him details: "I come up with story lines from dreams and real life people and experiences. It's important to define the characters personalities so people really get to know the people and develop feelings for them. Sometimes they are liked, sometimes they are villains and are hated, but you want readers to feel like they are real people. That's why the dialogue has to feel natural too." She also let him know that, "writing is a pretty long process, taking several months, maybe even a year to complete a book of 70,000 to 100,000 words, then there is editing and getting it published. It could be two years or so before we see the completed book. It can be done faster if you self-publish."

He shook his head in awe at her and said, "That's a lot. I never knew that it took so much effort and time. You must really be patient. And focused to get it all done the first time then write parts over to get it right. You do all of this by yourself? My hats off to you for your fortitude. I see why getting a publisher is such a big deal. Congratulations again." She felt that Panther Heat rise in her. No man she had ever been with wanted to know about writing or her books. It was sexy to her and added a dimension to his character that he really listened and asked her questions.

When Robert came home on Wednesday, he pulled Pat out of the kitchen again to dance, this time to Stevie Wonder's *Always*. The dance ended with her close in his arms and they paused to look at each other, both silently thinking that their bodies fit perfectly together and they danced like they had been dancing with each other all of their lives. She asked how he learned to dance so well. "My mom and Shelly. They said there was nothing classier and sexier than a man who knew how to move around a dance floor so we practiced a lot. Were they right?" he asked. He also remembered some of his college friends saying women believed that a good dancer was a good indication of whether a man was good in bed. He didn't mention that to Pat. Not the time for that conversation yet.

She blushed and tried to pull away to go back to the kitchen to finish dinner, but he held on to her until she responded. "Were they right?" He asked again.

"Mm-hmm." She mumbled in agreement, grinning so hard he knew she was impressed. He pinched her nose then let her go, heading to the bedroom to change clothes and come back to help with dinner.

Robert pressed her for a book update on Thursday, wanting to know the book title and what it was about. She looked quite serious when she told him, "The title is *Leap of Faith* and it's about two people who meet and get married on the same night." They both laughed. Robert was quick to say, "See, I told you when we met that you might get something to write about. Is it a happy ending?" to which Pat replied, "Don't know. Give me time. Have to write the story." They laughed again. Robert said he thought all the romance books had a happy ending so he was really looking forward to this one.

Pat then shared her real storyline: "Walter is an

English professor at a state university who attends a conference on teaching theories in Chicago when he meets Gloria, a history professor. They click right away and spend the last two days of the conference going to the sessions and having dinner together. The conversation stayed in his comfort zone, talking about the conference and their own teaching theories and experiences. They exchanged numbers before the end of the conference, and then when he got home, he realized he had an uncharacteristically strong interest in her. He had dated his share of women, but this woman was special and he wanted to romance her, not just give her his old lines that worked on other women, especially because she lived in another state. Long distance conversations and texts would not be enough. Then he remembered the love letters and cards he found that his dad had sent to his mom when they first met so he decided to go through them and use some for inspiration. It's a love story from a man's point of view."

Robert liked the idea and asked her to read some of the letters to him. She said when she was ready she would prefer he read them since it was a male perspective. He liked the idea of being involved in her work so he agreed, and said he would try not to pester her for updates.

Their first date night was sexy and fun. It was a Friday night so he changed out of his business suit into dark blue dress slacks and a long sleeved white shirt with a blue and white pinstripe sports jacket then went to the family room to make calls while she got ready. She took her que from his attire and wore a slim fitted white dress and a pair of open toed navy blue heels. It was a subtle hint that they were together without being dressed alike. They went to *Adelmo's Ristorante* in Dallas whose extensive Italian menu gave them both what they wanted to eat. She was excited and complimented him on the choice of restaurant because the warm bread and olive oil then the angel hair pasta with chicken were all delicious. During and at the end of the meal she moaned and licked her lips. He watched her, remembering how she moaned and squealed at *Willie G's*, where they first met, now she was moaning at *Adelmo's*. He was getting antsy to hear those noises in romantic situations with him. 'Patience' he kept repeating to himself as he willed his body to calm down. After dinner they took a drive around the area so that she could become familiar with some of his favorite places.

The rest of the week-end they got to know more about each other by playing 'getting to know you' games, like 'favorites,' 'best,' and 'worst ever.' They started at the grocery store on Saturday, identifying what foods they liked.

"What's your favorite meal?" Pat asked. "I noticed at *Willie G's* that you ordered a little bit of everything: the chicken and sausage gumbo and salad, then salmon for your entree. You did something similar on our date last night. Is that your typical meal combination?"

He admitted he was hungry on his birthday from missing lunch to get to Houston, and he enjoyed the food at *Adelmo's*, but the truth was he just liked to eat — meat, seafood, vegetables, pasta, potatoes, all of it. He didn't have any particular favorites. "I try to eat healthy most days, but I do have a sweet tooth. You know 7UP Cake is my favorite. However, I also love lemon pies, sweet potato pies, and a good peach cobbler. Maybe you can help me with that." He was looking at her lips and licking his. She blushed.

"Are you one of those salad and smoothie women? Don't want to gain five pounds so you don't eat except on special date nights or other occasions?" He was looking at her body while he asked the question.

"Trust me, I like to eat. Mostly chicken and turkey. But I have to have bacon and pork chops and a good burger every now and then. I like most vegetables too. And I don't have to tell you about pasta… as you saw I love pasta with olive oil and good warm bread. I have to go to the gym to help burn off those calories." She got a dreamy eyed look and he made a comment. "One day you might not need the gym. I can help you burn off those calories." He gave her that sexy smile again and she put her head down and smiled then shook her head, walking off towards the chips and cookies. They raced to pick their favorite snacks. Surprise, surprise, hands down for them both—ridged potato chips, popcorn, and chocolate chip cookies.

At home later that night, they fought over the remote and discussed what to watch. They both loved *Shawshank Redemption* and all of the *Oceans* and *Godfather* movies, so with any kind of drama or action movie it was going to be a good '*Netflix* and chill' night.

He shared with her, "I watch science fiction and super

hero movies but only with TJ or my male friends. I used to try to watch with women, but they were not really interested, just wanted to be with me, and asked too many questions or appeared bored so I stopped taking dates to those movies."

When she asked, his look confirmed that he definitely was not into romance movies or romantic comedies, but he promised to watch some with her.

On Sunday they live streamed the Wheeler Avenue Baptist Church service and Robert's alto voice sang all the songs as he remembered his choir days. Pat was a soprano. Her voice was soft and she had a good tone so they started practicing harmonizing together. That led to a discussion about favorite music. They both liked all types of music but agreed that aside from gospel music, R&B was the best, especially the way they played it on *Pandora* and *Sirius XM Soul Town* and *Silk*. She shared with him that "Smooth jazz is the backdrop to my writing life. It's soft, not distracting and very relaxing. Don't be surprised if you hear it all day if you are home, especially Brian Culbertson and Keiko Matsui." He smiled and confirmed that he liked it too so he was okay with hearing it a lot.

They also talked at length about God, church, religion, and spirituality. Of course they both believed in God and had seen and felt His presence in their lives. They acknowledged that they were both blessed with great parents and extended families, good health, and work that they loved, and they relied on their spirituality especially in dealing with death and healing from the losses.

They talked about favorite scriptures. His was Psalm 34:17 and 18: "The Lord hears his people when they call to him for help. He rescues them from their troubles. The Lord is close to the brokenhearted; he rescues those who are crushed in spirit." One of Pat's favorites was Philippians 4:13: "I can do all things through Christ who strengthens me."

She shared with him: "I completely understood when you said you heard God's voice the night we met. I have heard His voice too, and I have seen other 'signs and wonders' of God at work.

"When my mother died I was devastated and felt so completely alone, even in a room full of family and friends. After everyone left and I had the first afternoon by myself, I sat in a chair in the living room at the window, crying my heart out, asking God what was I going to do."

"I kept hearing a tap on the window that would not go away. Tap, tap, tap. Tap, tap, tap. Finally I got agitated. This noise was interfering with my sorrow. When I turned to see what was making the noise it was a big dark brown bird with orange on his chest who had built a nest on the ledge. A nest that I had never noticed before. Inside the nest was another bird, smaller, and brown with an orange chest too.

"I almost passed out in shock. It was a freezing cold day in February and usually all birds had flown South long before that time. Why were these two still around? Then I thought about the fact that birds were my mom's favorite animal and she had quite a few pictures and statues of birds around the house. She loved their beauty and the way they were so free to soar and spread their wings.

"I knew immediately that God was sending me the message that she and my dad were together and watching over me. It was affirmation that He would give me strength to survive the loss and find my way to a great future. That's when Jeremiah 29:11 became my other favorite scripture: 'For I know the plans I have for you declares the Lord. Plans to prosper you and not to harm you. Plans to give you hope and a future.'"

Robert spoke about his church history: "The McKnight family went to St. Johns Methodist Church regularly. Mom was involved with several groups. Dad was on the board of Trustees. Shelly and I joined the young adult choir and were members of the youth group where we had outings with other young Christians from other churches."

Pat's church history was similar. "My mom took me to New Covenant Baptist church while dad worked. Week-ends were his best earning days, when people were home from their regular jobs. Mom and I went to Bible study on Wednesdays and participated in most of the church events for families."

Out of those experiences, they both said they developed their beliefs and faith. Pat called herself more spiritual than religious because while she enjoyed, and sometimes needed the formal Sunday service, she was not dependent upon the church and the many groups and programs for nourishment and enrichment. Her attendance was about twice a month, and sometimes less often. She read books and watched a variety of ministers on television to reinforce and continue to develop her faith.

Robert preferred the church experience, just couldn't be consistent because of his work so he went when he could and supplemented with his own studying and watching ministers broadcasts.

They both noticed through the years, more and more scandals about various churches were in the news: married pastors dating members, money being stolen or some kind of fraud, more focus on the pastors' comfort and income than saving souls. They were disappointed but not undaunted, agreeing to find a church home and keep a watchful eye out for any people or practices that took away from their Christian experience.

That night they also opened up about their 'worst ever.' Both said it was the death of their parents. Before they went to sleep she asked him for his 'best ever.'

"Meeting you. And that's not a line. I know a lot of people, but I'm really a loner. You make me happy every day. I like coming home to you."

"Me too," Pat admitted, then they both snuggled closer and drifted off to sleep. It had been a great and fun week. They were excited about this being just the beginning for their lives together.

CHAPTER TWELVE

The boxes in the garage were bothering Pat. Robert had been living there for about six months but never took the time to unpack them. Pat guessed that he was waiting for the 'wife' and to figure out how to integrate his belongings in with hers once she moved in.

It was difficult to get to the Audi Pat drove and the way the boxes were stacked they looked like a big wall. She asked Robert if she could unpack them for him since she was home most of the day. You can learn a lot about a man when you go through what he keeps.

He did not hesitate, saying "Okay. But are you are sure you're ready to learn all about me? Maybe I should be here with you to make sure you don't run away when you find out who I really am."

Pat wasn't sure if he was joking or not since he didn't smile when he looked at her. Her antennae went up, wondering if she should be worried. She was learning about his dry sense of humor and she needed to figure out how to know when he was joking or testing her for a response. She looked at the boxes and hesitated, not sure if she should get started. Then she looked back at him and saw him smile and knew he was teasing.

The next day when Robert went to work she got started. Most of the boxes had a lot of paper—financial documents, keepsakes from work and Shelly and TJ, family pictures. But by the time she got half way through the boxes Pat knew he was a keeper—solid financially, a family man, no miscellaneous pictures of women or love letters or mementos.

It was the last few boxes that told the real story of the McKnight's. They were a family of understatements. What Pat was told at dinner the night she met the family was that dad was a cop, mom was a pediatric nurse, Shelly was an emergency room nurse, and Robert was an accountant.

The truth, as revealed in the boxes, was that their dad had been a special agent and an Intelligence Analyst for the FBI; their mom was in charge of women's health and maternity at Memorial Hermann, one of the highly recognized member institutions of the Texas Medical Center; and Shelly was the Director of Nursing at the Memorial Hermann Level 1 trauma center. The other interesting piece of information was that Robert might not just be an accountant. He had papers reflecting his own ties to the FBI but Pat was not sure if that was in the past or still current. She was impressed with all that they had accomplished, individually and as a family.

When Robert got home that night, he explained: "I had been a Forensic Accountant for the FBI for about five years before my parents died one night in a car accident. It was crazy because my dad had been in several dangerous undercover assignments year after year and never got shot or hurt in any way. Mom was just overcoming a breast cancer scare and they were out celebrating when they were hit by a drunk driver.

"I lost my anchors to the world and for a long time could not see how to get a firm grip on life. Shelly had Tommy and TJ so she didn't need me. I felt very alone. I took a leave from the FBI because it reminded me too much of my dad and all that he taught me and all that we shared. I didn't work for a few months and went a little wild in the streets. A lot wild with women and having sex as I told you.

"Then two of my best friends in the FBI, Howard Hunter and Frank Griffin, approached me about starting the company. Once it got going I buried myself in work. I co-own Executive Accountants with Howard and Frank. We trained together and have been close ever since. I consider them my brothers.

"We have each worked in different parts of the country so between the three of us we know the tax laws by region. Our primary client is the government. We are still considered active agents and maintain our credentials and security status.

"We also take high profile insurance and criminal cases and divorce cases of the ultra-rich, especially when one spouse is looking for any hidden assets. Much of our business is referrals from people who know about us and our reputation for being good at what we do. We find the money."

In addition, Robert said that he and his dad were well known at the FBI Academy in Quantico, Virginia and among other agents as the number one sharpshooters in their respective classes. When Pat mentioned to Robert the awards she found, he talked about his dad teaching him about guns and how to shoot. Then he took Pat to the master bedroom closet where there was a large safe in the back, housing the cache of weapons he and his dad had accumulated through the years.

Pat asked if he would take her to the gun range with him sometime so she could see him in action and learn to shoot. He was surprised that she wanted to learn, commenting, "most women I know are afraid of guns, but I think this is a great idea and fun for us to do together since shooting is something I really like to do."

Robert made it a point to emphasize that they were not allowed to publicize that he is an agent and asked that Pat not tell anyone. "It's important to maintain our anonymity for security reasons. There are crazy people out there who sometimes don't care who they kill as long as it's a government worker, especially law enforcement. So I'm an accountant to everyone. Not even TJ knows yet. The staff at our company got security clearances but were told that it was because of the need for security for the government contracts."

It was a lot to take in. Pat admired who they were and what they did. They were a serious, accomplished family, yet Shelly and Robert were fun and loving. Even in tragedy, the family bond was strong. In its own weird way this also confirmed that she could believe Robert meant it when he said he loved her and would take care of her. She felt she could finally relax and 'enjoy the ride' as her mom said.

CHAPTER THIRTEEN

At the end of the month, Pat met Robert's college buddies at their regular post-tax season gathering. Vivian was the youngest and single. Brian was single because of divorce. Charlotte and Jeffrey had not yet married. Jerome married Joann right after graduation. Sandy eventually married Gerald. Both couples had kids.

The location varied based upon what was going on in their lives. This time it was at the local pool and gaming hall with a bar where you could also order burgers, chicken wings, and French fries.

They called Robert "CB" for choirboy, saying that not only did he sing in the school choir, he was a clean, wholesome kind of guy and good friend. He was not the campus man whore that some of them were and he could have been because the ladies loved him. And they said he had always been quiet and private.

They were all stunned at Robert and Pat's story but were happy for them and wished them well. Except for one woman. There is always one.

Vivian had a crush on Robert from the moment he started hanging out with her brother Jerome. When everyone left the table to shoot pool, play games, or go to the bar, Robert asked her to sit so they could talk. He insisted Pat stay. He wanted to make sure Vivian was okay after learning that he was married.

He was sensitive to her feelings for him, reminding her that while she was a wonderful person, he had always considered her Jerome's little sister and a little sister/friend to him. He said he had told her that through the years when he was dating other women.

She acknowledged that what he said was truth, but had kept hope alive anyway. "My fault for never giving up" was how she put it. She respected him though, especially now that he had a wife, and asked Pat to "just let me hate you for a moment until I can pull my big girl panties up and move on."

They all laughed and hugged and Pat prayed for strength because she knew that there probably were more stories like this to come. She hoped they would all have such a good ending. What she didn't know was that there was another story to be told the same night.

Robert caught up with some of the guys at the pool tables. Vivian and Pat went to the ladies room and when they came out, they found seats near the pool tables and watched ladies make their way over to the guys, especially Robert. When the women tried to whisper in his ear he would back away and wave his hands as if saying 'no, I'm good, don't need that.'

Vivian, Charlotte, and Joann decided to go bowling and meet back with the guys in an hour for dinner. They made Pat feel welcome and a part of the group, not just Roberts's new wife, so she bowled with them.

The dinner table talk was fun and loud with the guys teasing over who was the best pool player. Food and drinks were ordered and just as the food came, a lady walked up and stood next to Robert. She nodded at the group then said, "Well, well, well Mr. McKnight. I thought you had fallen off the face of the earth."

Robert looked up at her and spoke. "Hello Lynnette." She did not move. "We need to talk Robert."

"About what?" He was frowning but not looking at her.

"I think we need to have that conversation away from your friends." She pulled on his arm.

"What is it Lynnette? I am busy here." He did not want to be rude, but he had nothing to say to her.

She leaned over and whispered in his ear and immediately all the blood drained from his face. He jumped up and said to Pat, loud enough for all to hear, "I'll be back." With that he pushed Lynnette toward the bar and they sat at a table. Pat looked at her watch, noting the time, then looked at the group to see if anyone knew her or what she might want with Robert. They all shook their heads. None of them seemed to know her.

For the next thirty minutes you could see Robert and Lynnette talking, ordering a drink, and talking some more. Jerome saw Pat getting anxious and went over to Robert. "Hey man, your food is getting cold." Robert waved him away, saying he would be there in a minute.

Ten minutes later Vivian went over to the table to ask Robert to come back to the table. The mood had shifted dramatically and everyone was looking at Pat to see what she was going to do. Robert didn't even look up at Vivian and said "I'll be there in a minute."

Pat could not eat as she watched Robert with the lady so she had their food wrapped up and put in a bag then she walked over to the table. She paused for a moment to see if he would look up but he did not. Finally she asked Robert if he was ready to go. He was looking on his cell phone and didn't look up but responded with a very agitated voice, "I said give me a minute."

Pat responded, hoping he would look up "You want another minute on top of the forty five you have already had sitting here?"

Robert looked up. His eyes had a weird look, as if he was looking at someone standing in front of him but not seeing who it was or that it was Pat.

"Yes, do you mind?" His tone was firm and dismissive and Pat read it loud and clear.

She put the bag with his food on the table and said "Not at all. Take your time." When she looked at the woman sitting with Robert, the woman had a very smug look on her face. Pat didn't have a clue about who she was or what had Robert so engrossed, but she knew the look of a woman who felt she had secured her man. Pat decided in that moment that it was time to leave the restaurant. And Robert.

Pat went back to the table with the rest of the group to say goodnight. "It was great meeting you all. I'm going to head out. Have a good night."

They all looked over at Robert and saw that he was not moving and started talking at once, asking if Pat needed a ride.

"I'm good thanks." She replied as she pushed the app on her phone for an Uber.

A tall, older man appeared next to her, walking in lockstep and started talking. "I'm Steve, security here. I've been watching you all night. You're very beautiful and don't deserve to be treated like that. May I get you a ride to wherever you want to go?"

"No thanks, I've got one coming." She was walking fast so that she could get as far away as possible as quickly as possible.

"Then I'll wait outside with you if that's ok. It's getting late." He was watching her and noticed that she wasn't sad or crying.

"Sure," Pat replied, her mind racing a mile a minute.

"Are you okay? You don't seem upset." He was surprised. "Most women would be hysterical or still inside starting a fight."

"Oh, I'm upset. But my mama always taught me to use my anger and frustration to be smart. I am strategizing in my head on my next move. I can cry another day.

He gave her his card. "Call me if you need me. For anything."

Pat took the card, read out loud "Steve Wilson, CEO, Networked Securities," smiled at him, and said thanks just as her ride was pulling up. As she got in, she heard Robert calling her and running toward the car. Steve stopped him to allow her time to pull off, asking Robert who he was and what did he want with the lady who just got in the car.

Robert told him to mind his business and ran to his

SUV, hoping to catch up to the car Pat was in before it left the parking lot but he was too late. He sped home, praying that she was headed there. He called her phone but kept getting her voice mail so he would leave a message, hang up, then call right back.

CHAPTER FOURTEEN

When he got to the house the overhead lights were on in addition to the lamps that they had on timers so he knew she was there. Once inside he noticed her key fobs he had given her for the cars were on the counter. She usually kept them in her purse. He knew that was a bad sign. He could hear her singing.

Robert knocked on the door to her room and pushed it open, noticing that she had already dismantled her office and was in the closet packing her clothes. She knew he was in her room but never stopped singing or packing. He asked her if they could talk.

"I'm busy. Maybe later." She replied without looking at him.

He walked toward her to get her to stop packing but stopped when she looked at him.

"And please don't come in here. I smell a woman's cologne on you and it's not mine."

Her eyes, usually warm and loving and smiling at him, were blank, cold, devoid of emotion. It took his breath away and he stumbled back out of the room. While he had looked at people like that, no one had ever looked at him that way before. She didn't look angry or sad. He knew it meant that she was not interested in him or anything he had to say. Ever again.

Now it was his turn to strategize. He knew he had screwed up royally and it was a very long shot to believe that she would want to be with him. But he had to try. She had become such an integral part of his life already that he was frightened of what would happened if they didn't end up together. He ran to the shower to wash off the offending scent and went back to the kitchen to wait for her.

An hour later, she came out of the room to get a bottle of water and Robert was waiting for her. She paused to ask drily, "What do you want Robert?"

"Would you please sit with me so we can talk? I need to tell you what happened tonight and it will take a minute." He gestured for her to sit by him at the counter.

"I'm good Robert." Pat responded, still standing. "And give me the cliff notes version. I don't need all the gory details."

He took a deep breath and started. "The woman at the restaurant is Lynnette and I was spending time with her for a couple of months before my parents died. Not really dating just...you know, having sex. I was not interested in her. Then my parents died and I stopped all contact. Tonight was the first time I've seen her in five years. She whispered in my ear that she has a son. My son. It totally freaked me out, to see her after so long and hear that I might have a son. So I wanted to get as much information as possible from her which is why we went to the bar area to talk. I don't believe her son is mine and when you guys were trying to get my attention I was trying to find a place to get DNA tests as quickly as possible to know for sure."

Pat finished her water and as she was throwing the bottle away said, "Congratulations Robert. Now you have the family you said you wanted." She headed back to her room thinking so that's why the woman had a smirk on her face. Having his child was definitely a trump card so she would always have a place in his life.

Robert ran in front of Pat before she could get to the door. "I don't believe that child is mine. I always wore condoms. Always. Have since college. Even though she said she was on birth control I still took no chances. I definitely didn't want a baby then. And definitely not with her. So I found a place for us to get tested tomorrow and we will know for sure in a few days."

He waited for Pat to say something or even look at him. She did neither. She walked around him to go into her room. He walked in behind her. "Come on. Don't leave me. I'm really sorry that I got so caught up I didn't realize how much time had passed and I didn't see you when you asked me to go. I was terrified and needed to do what I could to get things straight with her tonight. Don't go."

Pat sat in the chair that had been at her makeshift desk and turned on her iPad. Since it was too late to get a flight back to Houston she secured an Enterprise rental car online and they were picking her up in the morning at ten. She just had to get through the night and she was going to do that in her room.

Robert had more to say. "I know you're mad and you have every right to be. I'm sure I'll regret this night for a long time, but we need to work through this. It's our first fight and it's a big one. But we can get through this."

Pat looked up at him with a question in her eyes. "What makes you think I'm mad at you Robert? I'm not mad at you. I'm disappointed. I thought we were trying to work toward something but I was clearly wrong. Tonight I was very quickly dismissed by you so it told me that our relationship holds little meaning. I felt devalued. And for it to happen in front of her and all of your friends was demeaning. I just felt dirty, like I didn't belong with you and now she and your college friends know it too."

She paused then continued. "I've been learning a lot about you every day Robert. Tonight I learned that certain things take your full attention and I shouldn't expect you to see me as a priority. Or even a factor. So I'm not angry with you. I'm angry with myself. For trusting you, believing that this handsome, sexy, charismatic, thoughtful man who clearly has his pick of women would stay focused on me. It's been an interesting interlude with you Mr. McKnight, one I'll never forget. Thank you for the lesson on not being so gullible, even when you think God is telling you something. The devil also speaks.

"I'll be out of your way in the morning so if it's okay I'm going to stay tonight. If that's a problem for any reason, I'll get a ride and be out of your way in a half hour. What would you prefer?" Her voice was as cold as the look in her eyes. Very matter of fact, no emotion.

"I don't want you to go at all. Stay so we can work through this. I am sorry. I have never been so stupid with someone I care about." He had to think about how to keep them together. Robert sat watching Pat through the open door. She read for about an hour then made the decision to stay in the room for the night. This was her private space, a sanctuary and she didn't want to sleep with Robert or on the sofa in the family room. With no bed or comfortable chair in the room, she laid on the carpeted floor with a pillow and blanket and went to sleep. She was exhausted, mentally and physically.

He went in the room and laid down next to her, getting as close as possible without waking her up. While she slept, he prayed until he too fell asleep.

CHAPTER FIFTEEN

In the morning he acted like it was a typical Saturday morning for them, getting breakfast started before she got up and waited for her to get dressed. He fixed his creamy cheese grits that she loved along with sausage and eggs and toast. She was hungry since she did not eat at the restaurant the night before so she ate breakfast but had nothing to say to him but thanks when she was done.

He was chattering away through the whole meal about the weather and what Shelly had to say on their call earlier. He casually asked where she was getting a car from and she said Enterprise. He knew immediately what to do.

Robert went into the bedroom to get dressed and called Enterprise, saying his wife had ordered a car because she thought he had to work and couldn't take her where she needed to go but plans had changed. One night while she was sleeping he had made copies of her drivers license and credit cards, needing them for some papers she would have to sign once she signed the marriage license so he was able to cancel her car rental. When he came out she was looking out the window for the Enterprise valet. He asked her not to get mad then told her that he had cancelled her car and he would take her back to Houston. "I brought you here, I should at least be the one to take you back. It's the least I could do."

Pat did not ask how he had cancelled her reservation. She figured as an agent he could do a lot of stuff the average person could not do. She really didn't care as long as she could go home. Robert was glad she was okay with that. He needed to stay with her as much as possible so he packed a bag. He told her he had a call to be on and they could head out. It was a Zoom call with all of the friends at dinner the night before. He had arranged it that morning while cooking. He asked her to sit next to him at the island for the call but she refused, instead standing off to the side to see what this was about. They could not see her but Robert told them she was standing by.

"Thanks everybody for getting on the call this morning. I'll be quick. I wanted to apologize to all of you for leaving the table so abruptly last night after Lynnette came up, and for being so testy when you were trying to get my attention in the bar. One day I'll tell you what that was about. In the meantime, the most important reason for the call is to apologize to Pat in front of all of you for being so stupid and rude to her. We have talked and I have apologized to her but I also wanted to apologize to her in your presence. I don't want any of you to think that I don't care about her or that she deserves to be treated so terribly. She is the woman I plan to spend the rest of my life with if I can get her to forgive me for last night. And she probably won't even consider that if she believes that you guys think that she is not the fabulous, sexy woman who makes my heart beat. So I'm sorry for being such a jerk and I pray that Pat will one day forgive me and we can all get together again."

No one said a word initially, then they all started talking at once. "You were a jerk CB man."

"How could you do that to her? She's a sweetheart. We want her in our group. You go find another group."

"Pat should leave you alone until you grow up and can handle your business better."

"Hey Pat, divorce him and take all of his money. That will teach him."

While they were talking he kept his eyes on Pat and his mouth was saying 'I'm sorry.' She was looking at them and half smiling at their comments. When she looked at him the disappointment showed on her face and she walked to the garage to put her bags in the car. He hung up and closed the house up to leave. He was not sure when he would be back. What he did know was that he was not coming back without her.

Instead of heading for the highway he told her they first needed to make the stop at the medical facility for the DNA test. He asked her to come in with him. "I want you with me throughout this process. If he is not mine, then we will know and can keep working on us. If he is mine, then we can discuss how it will affect our relationship, with finances, visitation, everything. Look at it this way; if nothing else you can wipe that smug look off of Lynnette's face when she sees us together. I know it's silly, but I need her to see us together and know that you are important to me and she can't come between us, child or no child."

Pat didn't say anything but she got out of the car. She thought it was silly too, a bit twisted even, but decided she deserved one last moment to feel special.

They were the first to arrive. When Lynnette and her son got there, Robert and Pat both looked at him for any physical similarities. There were none. Not a hairline or hair color or eyes or dimple. The McKnight genes were strong so there had to be something familiar. Nothing. Both of them exhaled softly.

He introduced Pat as his wife and Lynnette's face fell. "You didn't mention that you were married last night. When did this happen?" She was clearly not smirking now.

"On my birthday, May 10th." Robert was smiling and looking at Pat so sincerely. Pat was looking at Lynnette with a look of empathy for her that said, 'don't be so quick to think you've got all the cards.'

Lynnette introduced her son and they all went back to the room for the blood test. The results would be available and emailed no later than Wednesday.

Robert and Pat headed for Houston. She was still not talking to Robert so he drove in silence, continuing to plan his next move with her. The closer they got to Houston the more relaxed she became. She looked out the window and after a while fell asleep.

She woke up in Shelly and Tommy's driveway. Robert said he would only be a minute and asked her to come in. She shook her head no. Shelly came out to her while Robert talked to Tommy and TJ.

"Robert told me what happened. I'm sorry Pat. How are you?" Shelly wanted to hug her and ask her to forgive Robert but knew that was not her place.

"I'm good Shelly. Just want to be home. Hoping there are no more stops to make."

Robert came back just then and said they had to go. The next stop was the grocery store. He wanted to make sure she had food since she had been away for a few weeks so he filled up the basket with breakfast and dinner foods. She kept saying she didn't need all of that but he insisted.

At her building, they got a cart for all of the food and her suitcases; then the doorman and Robert loaded it up. Pat parked the car while Robert took the cart to her place. When she got there, she noticed Roberts bag and asked Robert why it was in her apartment. His only response was that he was tired and needed to rest. She was conflicted, understanding that it had been a long drive and a long day so she understood that he was tired, but also wanting him to leave so she could get her single, working life in Houston started up again.

That night sleeping in her own bed was bittersweet. Robert was on the couch and she was missing him and yet still disappointed in the turn of events. She fell asleep but started dreaming and crying. Robert heard her and went to the door of her bedroom. She did not respond to him calling her name so went over to the bed. She was asleep so he climbed into bed with her and wrapped his body around her. It calmed her and she stopped crying. She never woke up.

The next morning, Sunday, Robert was up fixing breakfast when Pat came out of the bedroom. She was watching him, noting how he was acting like nothing was wrong between them. When she asked him when he was leaving, he gave her a long look and shrugged then talked about the weather and what they forgot at the store and what she wanted for dinner.

It finally dawned on her that this was Robert's stubborn side. He was going to stay with her until she gave in to him and went back with him. This is what Shelly meant when she said Robert knew how to get what he wanted and always did.

She went back into the bedroom to let that sink in. She was torn between wanting to love him and being sad about the way he handled the child situation and knowing that to go back meant he would probably do something like that again. She got a headache thinking about it and decided to just let things play out over the next few days.

On Sunday and Monday they both worked from her apartment, and at night he continued to sleep on the couch until he heard her crying in her sleep. She woke up on Tuesday morning in his arms and knew for sure her theory was right. She asked him directly, "Will you please leave Robert? I need to call in for some work days and get back to my life."

He looked in her eyes when he answered. "I'll leave whenever you are ready to go back with me. I have some work to do to get you back on track toward loving me, but right now I would be happy if you just didn't cry in your sleep every night."

The interesting thing was both of them were thinking about making love. He believed it would be helpful to win her over if he could romance her, including making love, but he had to settle for staying with her, cooking and talking and not letting her out of his sight, hoping that their natural rhythm together would help heal them.

She wanted to know what it would feel like for him to make love to her. He was so sexy and sleeping with him was getting harder and harder to do without turning over and attacking him. She wasn't a virgin and it had been a long time since the last time with a man. Why not have one night together before he went back to Dallas and out of her life?

CHAPTER SIXTEEN

Early on Wednesday the DNA results were in Robert's email. When he saw where the email was from, he sat on the sofa and pulled Pat into his lap so they could open and read it together. The results confirmed his belief. Lynnette's son was not his. He held on tightly to Pat, thanking God and whispering in her ear, "Please let us get back to where we were. I promise not to do dismiss you again with another woman or in any other way. Ever. I need you."

She felt the same way she did the first night they met. Then she was caught up in his Panther Heat. Drawn to him and excited to explore life with him. Now her feelings were mixed up with liking him after being together these few weeks. Except for that one horrible night, he had treated her with so much love and respect, she felt like a beloved wife to him. She really loved being with him. Truthfully, she loved him. She wanted to say yes, but she was so afraid that he would hurt her again. It was a very familiar feeling.

She tried to pull away but he held onto her until it was time to cook dinner. When they went to bed that night, he held her especially close and even throughout the night. He prayed that if he had any kind of sex appeal or magnetism with women he wanted God to use all of it tonight to get her back.

The next morning he admitted, "I brought the marriage certificate with me. Today would be a good day for you to sign it and we could leave it with Tommy to file." He looked at her as if he would explode if she didn't sign. She smirked and said "No, not today Robert."

"Is it something you will still consider?" He wanted her to say she wanted him too.

"Robert. You dismissed me. In public. That doesn't go away in less than a week over breakfast and a couple of dinners."

He held her hand and rubbed her arm. "I know. You are right. I was just hoping. Boy, you are stubborn. I can see who will keep our kids in line. Okay. I'll beg you some more. I have no shame. The problem is you need to sign the papers so we can have make-up sex."

Pat had to smile at that. He was still holding her and she knew he could feel her weakening.

"Okay, how about this: You sign now and we can wait until we get back home to make love in the king size bed. That bed of yours is small for a big man like me. I need room to move around. I'll wait. Okay?"

Pat was non-committal. "Robert, if you need to get back to Dallas to work, I understand. We can talk on the phone."

He burst out laughing. "I am working while I'm here so don't try that. Remember, I don't do long distance. And besides, I'm not leaving here without you. So curse at me, hit me, beat me up, get it all out of your system so you will be ready on Friday to go back to our home."

By the time Friday came, he had worn Pat down with his hugs and jokes, and he had them in the kitchen cooking and dancing together. She could not resist him.

Robert and Pat decided to stay in Houston through the week-end. They had a family dinner on Friday night with Shelly and Tommy and TJ at a soul food restaurant. Shelly and Tommy were very happy to see Robert and Pat working their way back together. Robert spent Saturday with TJ while Pat had lunch with friends then visited with Uncle Roy and Aunt Ginny. They closed up Pat's apartment and headed back to Robert's house on Sunday.

Life went back to their regular routine for the next several weeks, only Pat was still quietly looking for signs that something would go wrong again. Robert could tell so he was extra attentive to her to assure her of his love.

Their Friday dates were upbeat and fun. He took her to the gun range which allowed him to stand close behind her and put his arms around her so she would have the right stance and hold the gun properly. The booth was small and tight, so they felt each other's heat intensely. Once she got used to the kickback of the gun, her aim was controlled and direct. Robert especially liked when she hit the target in the head or the heart area. She would jump up and down and squeal and wiggle so close to him that he had to walk away to keep her from seeing or feeling the effect on his body. Celibacy was definitely becoming harder to maintain. After a series of shots where she unloaded the clip in rapid fire, she was so excited she squealed and turned to kiss him. He smiled and licked his lips and looked in her eyes. She paused, knowing that kissing would breach their agreement and change the course of their relationship. Were they ready for that when the marriage license still had not been signed? She was determined to hold out so she hugged him and turned back around, smiling because she felt his excitement for her when she leaned into him for the hug.

The next week they went to a crowded comedy club and got the last table for two, sitting very close together, holding hands under the table and talking in each others ear to be sure they were heard. They realized they each liked to critique the jokes that were not funny, which mostly came from the new comedians. They howled at the more seasoned storytellers and leaned on each other in a very familiar way.

A wine and art night the next week revealed their personalities through their color choices for the same scene being painted. He chose rich dark colors – black, brown, deep blues, dark green, burgundy, while she used more yellow, pink, white, light blues and greens. To Robert it showed that she was indeed a ray of sunshine, the light of his world, and radiating happiness that he loved. To Pat, it confirmed that he was grounded and serious but not sad or brooding, an anchor for her world so she could be free to be who she was and who she wanted to be.

CHAPTER SEVENTEEN

The Fourth of July weekend was coming up and Robert wanted to spend it with his family. He asked Pat if she was ok and if they were ok. She said yes to both. He was happy to hear that so he asked again that she give notice to her apartment management and have movers ready to pack her up and get her moved while they were there.

She couldn't do it. Not yet. She wanted to, but in her heart she knew it was still too soon. Not sure what she needed to see or hear or feel to be able to make the commitment, but she was not there yet. She had not signed the marriage license and he was visibly disappointed. They didn't talk for hours. She retreated to her room and he pretended to read but just stared at the book, never turning a page. Finally he went to her room and, without saying a word, pulled her up from the chair and led her to the kitchen. They sat facing each other on the island chairs and he took her hands in his.

"Talk to me Pat. Tell me what's going on. Am I doing something else wrong? Do you need me to do more of something? What is it? I'm not trying to rush you, it's just that every day when I leave here I wonder if you will be here when I get home.

"You have never actually said how you feel about me. I'm going on faith that since you came back with me a few weeks ago and you're still here that we have a chance. The closer it gets to the ninety days the more nervous I get. I am almost afraid to go to work. So tell me, what will it take to get you to commit to me? To us?"

Pat took a deep breath, looked into his eyes, and told him the truth. "I like you Robert. Very much. Except for the one hiccup, you have been a gentleman, very accommodating, and fun to be with and date. And I haven't slept this well since I was a baby."

"The truth is that "hiccup" was big to me. HUGE actually. It reinforced my fear of abandonment and I cannot get over the feeling that it was so easy for you to not see me when I'm standing right in front of you, asking you to come with me and not stay with her. It set me back to day one almost. It felt so cold and unfeeling to be treated like that.

"I get it, the possibility of you having a child, especially one that you didn't know about, is a big deal and it was a shock. Maybe if we had been together longer you might not have gotten so caught up. But you have been trained to react quickly in situations. I guess I didn't represent any danger so it was easy for you to carry on your business with her and ignore me.

"It reminded me of why my marriage was a big failure. I was not enough for him. He cheated and ignored me and I felt very alone. It's hard to jump back into a similar situation without taking some extra time to get to know you and see if it happens again.

"I need to be assured that I am somebody's number one for the long term. You make me feel so good and wanted and loved. But that hiccup was a good example that anybody can put on a show for a few weeks so I guess I need more time. I need some kind of assurance that you won't dismiss me again, cheat on me, or leave me so that I am alone again."

He looked at her long and hard, rubbing her hands. Finally, he said "Ok. I'll give you more time." Pat let her breath out slowly.

"Let me add, Robert that I promise to be here when you come home unless you give me reason to leave. And you will know if you have given me reason to leave. So please don't be anxious about that."

Then he confessed to her. "Truth? I am really loving you Pat. I love that you are here with me, that you are here when I come home at night, and that you are so engaged with life and the world around us, that you keep pulling me into your world and out of my shell. So I don't want to lose what we already have and what I imagine is to come. Definitely don't want to lose you. I still want what my parents had – a loving, fun, long term relationship. I have needed someone to love and someone to love me as number one too. So you don't have to worry about me dismissing you ever again, or cheating on you or leaving you. I have been praying for you for a long time and I am very glad that God finally answered and that His answer is you."

Pat knew she had less than six weeks left to decide and wanted every possible day to help her be sure. Even

Panther Heat couldn't fix everything could it?

They went to bed that night without getting much sleep, just holding each other. They went to Houston on Friday, returned on Sunday, then left on Monday for a few days at *Salamander Resort and Spa* in Middleburg, Virginia, then on to the *National Museum of African American History* in New York. Robert wanted them to have as much time together as possible, both to help Pat decide to sign the papers and to create good memories for when tax season came and he was not around as much.

It was right after that trip that Pat decided she was going to sign the marriage license. She knew that there was a lot more to learn about Robert and more for them to experience together, but she felt sure she wanted him so they might as well do it as a married couple.

She called Maggie to put in her notice that she was never coming back and that she was married. Maggie wished her well and said she would miss her and please stop by when she was in Houston. Pat had also called her apartment building management and emailed her written notice that she was vacating the apartment, and had secured movers with the promise to give them at least three days' notice. She was going to wait until the last possible minute to sign to keep Robert guessing, because she knew once the license was signed he would want to get her moved to Dallas. She was ready to make the transition, from single to married life and from Houston to Dallas.

CHAPTER EIGHTEEN

Day eighty-three was a dreary and dark Saturday. It was so close to the ninety-day deadline Robert had started believing that Pat was not going to sign the marriage license and he was disappointed. He was quiet throughout the morning, not wanting to ask if she realized the ninety days were almost up and if she had made up her mind. Instead, he asked what she wanted to do that day. She became really animated, giggling and dancing and saying, like a kid in a classroom with the right answer and trying to get the teachers attention, "I know, I know! Two things" then went running to their bedroom.

She came out with a Fed Ex envelope in her hand and slammed it down on the counter like a winning ace in bid whist. He looked puzzled. "What is this?" he asked, afraid to get excited that it was what he thought it was. He opened the envelope and it was the marriage license. She stood between his legs and took the pen he had used on the night of the ceremony and signed while he watched, then kissed him like he always kissed her: forehead first, then nose, right cheek, left cheek, and last a quick swipe on the lips. "I love you" she said, "and I am ready to be Mrs. Robert McKnight. Today. Right now. Until death do us part."

He was speechless. He leaned back on the island counter on one elbow and rested his other arm on the back of the chair. He looked at her for a long time then cleared his throat and asked, "Why now?"

She laughed and said, "Truth be told, God spoke to me too the day we met and said you were the answer to my prayers. I was very skeptical. You were so forward in the way you approached me and very bold in declaring your intentions, without even knowing me. It felt like I was being ambushed and you really frightened me. And then, even during our hiccup you never let me out of your sight.

"So when I think about what my mom said about knowing when I was with 'the one,' you made me feel exactly the way she described. You have been true to your word, taking really good care of me, making me fall in love with you every day. So it's time. And I didn't need another ceremony to start our married life."

He nodded, then said, "Tell me what your mom said."

"That the real love of my life would bring a Panther Heat, an intensity that no other man would have for me and I would feel only from him. And he would stalk me until I surrendered. You do that. You definitely bring the heat. And you know you are a stalker," she said with a raised eyebrow and a smile. "So I surrender to you now. Gladly."

He was shaking his head. "I like that. I have definitely been feeling the heat with you too. Panther Heat huh?

Your mom was a smart woman. Glad she got us to today."

She leaned into him, her hands on each side of his face and licked her lips then his lips, slowly pressing her lips onto his like she was sealing them together, then pausing, inhaling his breath. She was ready to start the sexual and sensual side of their married life, sliding the tip of her tongue into his mouth. He smiled and slowly opened his mouth to see what she would do. He did not move his tongue, while she licked the tip and went in search for the rest and exploring his mouth. He was watching her. She had her eyes closed. When she realized he wasn't kissing her back she stopped and opened her eyes. He pulled back from her to say, "I need to tell you something." She could not imagine what he wanted to say right NOW. "What is it?" She asked leaning in again so her lips were still touching his.

Robert whispered while he wrapped his arms around her and started moving his hands inside her top and pants to feel her body. "I have been mesmerized by your lips and tongue since we met. When you talk and when you eat and laugh and even when you pout in your sleep. Your mouth is so sexy to me. I already know that I'm going to like kissing you, so I'm going to be kissing you a lot. Like tongue and lips swollen, can't talk, can only text, a lot. Just wanted you to know that."

"Oh. Okay" she whispered. "I like kissing too so we're good."

With that, Robert pulled her to him and put his tongue in her mouth, kissing her like he had not had a kiss in years, pressing his tongue in then biting and licking her lips and her chin before driving his tongue in again. He kissed her dimples then sucked her tongue. He kissed her eyes and rained little kisses down the side of her face and around her ears and neck then made himself at home in her mouth for the next ten minutes. She was hungry for him too and pressed into him, fighting to imprint her tongue in his mouth too. They both started moaning and kissed as if nothing else in the world mattered. He could feel a blanket of warmth cascading down his body.

When they finally came up for air they smiled at each other and stayed close together, his lips touching her forehead, pausing but getting ready for more. He asked her to give him a second and moved her to sit in the chair next to him at the island. He went to the bedroom and brought out their favorite set of wedding rings from the store. What a surprise! He shared with her, "I ordered them about two weeks ago, believing that since the ninety days were fast approaching and you were still here then you would sign soon. Honestly though, I became very unsure in the last several days. It's not that many days left before the 90th day." He sounded almost sad.

She teased him. "Scared I was going to say no and go back home? Not a chance Mr. McKnight. You surrounded me and loved on me so hard that now I'm here to stay."

Robert said a prayer as he put her rings on her finger. "Thank you God. Thank you Jehovah Jireh, you have definitely provided for me with this woman. Thank you

Jehovah Rapha, for healing me from the loss and lack in my life so that I could be prepared for this day. Thank you for answering my prayer for a good woman. Thank you for Patricia. She's not just good, she's perfect for me, better than I ever imagined. Thank you."

He held her hands in both of his then looked into her eyes, saying, "And thank you Patricia Elaine Harris McKnight. For loving me and trusting me and allowing me to love you. You are beautiful and loving and kind and smart and fun and tolerant and all that I need. I pledge to spend the rest of my life with you. I commit to loving you, being faithful to you, caring for you, sharing with you, protecting you and providing for you in all the ways that God will allow. I love you so much and I intend to enjoy every moment of the rest of my life with you."

Pat put his ring on his finger then paused to look in his eyes and say "I love you Robert Allan McKnight. I came to you broken and afraid of love, afraid to trust. And you have been all of the man you promised to be to me and more. You have loved me back to wholeness and given me the heart to love you unconditionally. Every day I wake up trying to figure out what I ever did to deserve you and what I can do each day to show you how much I love you. I can't wait to see you at night so that we can share the adventures of our day. And I go to sleep each night nestled in your arms and knowing that I am loved like no one else could love me.

"Thank you Robert, for following God's voice and choosing me and loving me. I thank God for you every day. I love you with every fiber of my being. I promise to be faithful to you and grow with you and love on you until I have no breath left."

Together they said "Amen." Robert wrapped his arms around her and kissed her forehead and the dimples, and when he got to her lips, he licked her lips to make her open her mouth so he could slide his tongue inside again. Only this time their kiss was slow and tender, very seductive, their tongues slowly touching and exploring. They both moaned, happy to finally be able to have physical intimacy whenever they wanted.

Then he said really loud with pride: "I AM A MARRIED MAN." They danced to Rachelle Ferrell and Will Downing singing "*Nothing Has Ever Felt Like This*" and when the music stopped they just held each other, savoring the moment.

Shelly's call interrupted them and Robert told her the news. She screamed and called Tommy and TJ to the phone. They were all shouting "Congratulations! We love you Mr. and Mrs. McKnight! Robert and Patricia McKnight. Bobby and Pat McKnight." And singing *We Are Family.*

After they hung up, Robert asked Pat what she wanted to do to mark the occasion, "Do you want to leave today to go away on a honeymoon, fly or drive somewhere, or go to a special lunch or dinner, invite some friends and family to celebrate with us?"

Pat said no, slowly looking down his body, stopping at his waist and pulling on the waistband of his pants, and asked if those were things he wanted to do today. He smiled as he watched her looking at his body and pulling on his pants then said softly "no, not today." He shut off their cell phones, checked the kitchen to make sure everything was off, then picked her up and carried her into the bedroom.

He slowly laid her down on the bed and climbed in with her then kissed her ears and neck, and her cheeks again. His tongue opened her mouth and slid in. They explored each other's lips and mouths and tongues for what seemed like forever. Pat was finally free to explore his body and it felt good. Broad shoulders and tight butt and legs. He was solid and just a little hairy—chest, stomach, legs. Sexy.

He removed her top, licking and kissing and sucking her neck, shoulders, arms, and the palms of her hands. Her bra hooked in the front so she opened it for him, revealing her breasts one at a time. He smiled and said "Hello Ladies. I am really happy to finally see you."

Her nipples became hard in anticipation of his lips and tongue. He did not disappoint. He licked and kissed and bit softly all around each breast first, then sucked gently on her nipples. It was as if he had found his new home and was in no hurry to leave, going slowly from one nipple to the other. She started a low, steady moan in his ear and her hands rubbed his shoulders and back.

What he soon realized was that every time he sucked, a signal went directly down the center of her body and she could feel a throbbing between her legs and heat rising. She was wet and ready. He pulled her pants down and his tongue followed. Down one side and up the other, until his tongue reached what he later called 'his own personal juice box.'

To Pat, it felt like he was painting inside her with his tongue, brush strokes that drove her crazy. Some long and firm, others soft and light. The combination made her feel faint, her heart was racing and she kept whispering "Oh my God. That tongue. You are so good. This feels so good." She couldn't hold out any longer and called for Bobby in a low, breathless voice as she exploded.

He opened her legs wide and kissed the length of each of her thighs before he went back to stroking her with his tongue and sucking up her juice, still slowly, only this time with a little more pressure.

Pat had never felt anything like that before and asked him what he was doing. He stopped for a moment to say "I am signing my name so you will always know who you belong to and that I love you." Her second orgasm hit with such force she could only scream "Aaaaaahhhh." She could not form words. He kissed his way back up her body to her breasts and neck again.

Robert leaned over to the box under the bed to get a condom, watching her stretch and open her eyes to look at him. It had been a long time for her too so she wasn't used to that much attention. She needed a minute before she could engage in anything else.

Then she saw him totally nude for the first time. She felt the heat wash over her. Her nipples stood at attention once again and every place his tongue had been on her body was on fire.

Her mouth watered and she thought "Ooh. Happy Birthday to me." He smiled and said "to me too" so Pat guessed she really said it out loud. She had a flashback to the night they met when he said everything about him was big. He was right. A little longer than any she had ever seen, and definitely larger in circumference. He was big. For a long time Pat would salivate every time she saw him naked. In the old days it would probably be called swooning.

While putting on the condom, he looked at her as if to ask if she thought he was too big for her. She licked her lips and shrugged in anticipation. He moved inside her cautiously. They both moaned then paused to enjoy the feeling that they were finally together and how hot and tight and wet it felt.

First time sex is usually awkward. Not with them. They were already in sync. The sex was like him: intense and thoughtful. He was slow and deliberate as if he was memorizing the inside of her body inch by inch. She watched his face change from studied concentration to passionate beast. He paused after a few strokes to look into her eyes with a combination of love and lust that she had never seen before. It felt like their souls fused together in that moment.

"I love you Patricia McKnight. I need you. So much. And this?" He was moving inside her again. "I have dreamed of this every night since I met you. I am so hungry for you."

When he had every inch inside her, he raised up and stretched his arms out, reaching for hers hands along the way, then started rocking inside her. He had found his sweet spot and got very acquainted with hers. Pat knew she couldn't last much longer and she could feel him pushing harder and faster and muttering words like, "I, we, mine, yes, yes, oh, God." No coherent sentences.

She started moaning in his ear from somewhere deep in her soul, then starting calling for him. "Bobby? Bobby?" He slowly responded, "Yes baby, me too. I. Got. You." They were both pushing hard to get closer and closer to one another while feeling the force of their love explode inside her body. As his body calmed down, he kissed her tenderly on her neck and face, murmuring, "I love you. So much. You feel so good. I'm so happy."

When Robert tried to get up, Pat wrapped her arms and legs around his body, forcing him to stay in position. His weight felt so good, and he kissed her forehead and eyes and cheeks and lips.

All of a sudden she burst into tears, overwhelmed with the way he had made her feel. He was immediately concerned.

"What's wrong? Did I hurt you? What happened? Talk to me Pat. Say something."

She was crying hard and so embarrassed she couldn't look at him. "I'll be okay. Just give me a minute."

He looked frightened but waited until she stopped crying and could talk to ask again, "What is it Pat? Tell me."

She put a pillow over her face and said, "I'm sorry. I'm really embarrassed."

He took the pillow away then rolled off of her so that

they could sit up and have a conversation.

"What is there to be embarrassed about? It's just us. I am your husband. What is it?"

"First of all," she put her finger on his lips then ran her fingers down his chest as she explained. "That snake in your mouth and that Python between your legs, both need to be registered as lethal weapons and warning signs posted."

"I have NEVER, EVER been so thoroughly worked over and completely satisfied. Will you make love to me like this every time? It might send me to an early grave and I'm not leaving you here to give these goodies to anyone else."

He threw his head back, laughed really loud and blushed. She could tell he got a big ego boost from her comments and it was well deserved.

Then he acted so cool. "Okay, thank you, good to know, especially from Ms. Romance Writer, Ms. Sensual Experience expert. Too much for you?" He burst out laughing again. His curiosity got the best of him. "Then why the tears?"

After a heavy sigh, she explained. "Did you ever see the movie 'City of Angels' with Nicholas Cage and Meg Ryan?"

He looked puzzled and said, "No."

"No, of course not. It's a romance. Never mind. Anyway, in the movie, Nicolas Cage asks Meg Ryan 'what happens physically when we cry?' She's a medical doctor so she proudly gives him the technical answer: 'tear ducts operate on a normal basis to lubricate and protect the eye and when in emotion they overact and create tears.' But his response is what I'm feeling right now."

Robert was intrigued. "What is that?" he asked.

"Nicholas Cage said, "Maybe emotions become so intense your body just can't contain it. Your mind and your feelings become too powerful and your body weeps."

"I am weeping for you Robert. My body is weeping tears of joy for you. I love you so much, and every inch of my body adores every inch of yours. So that's why I'm crying."

He pushed her back on the bed and rolled on top of her, kissing her neck and face. He groaned saying "I don't know where you get all this stuff you come up with, but I like it. You are a smart and tasty delight. What am I going to do with you?"

"Love me like you just did!" she said very flippantly. "And we'll be good for life." They both chuckled.

She asked him if there was something else he wanted to do that day. He responded slowly, "No, we are staying home and I'm staying inside your body until you clearly understand that everything from here" he patted the top of her head then ran his hand down the side of her body to rub the bottom of her feet, "to here, is mine, only for me, no one else. Just like all of me is only and exclusively just for you. If you have a problem with that, speak now."

Patricia McKnight sealed that deal with a kiss. After what he had done to her, she knew no one else stood a chance.

They took a shower together and headed for the kitchen. They needed sustenance for this marathon. Periodically throughout the day, she could hear him say under his breath 'Lethal weapons. Snakes. Python. Her body weeps for me. Ha! My wife!'

At one point in the afternoon he looked at her and said, "So I've got to make your body weep? That's a pretty high bar. Don't expect that to happen every time." They both laughed.

When they finally came up for air that first night he asked her why she only called him Bobby when they were making love.

"Truth? I never liked nicknames for men. Usually they are stupid like Junior or June Bug or Big Boy. Bobby is different, it's a real name but it still feels weird. Somehow though, when you are doing what you do to me, it's hard to be so formal and call you *Robert*." She said his name in a very exaggerated and annoying nasal tone but with a smile.

He laughed and said he was ok with that being private, just for them. "When you call me Bobby in that soft, sexy low moan, I can hardly control myself. I know it's coming from deep inside you so that will let me know when I am doing my best, hitting the right spots for you.

"May I share something else with you?" He continued without waiting for an answer. "You know, I hear you moaning in your sleep when you are dreaming and I have had to get out of bed a few times and take a cold shower or find something to do to keep from ravishing you. On a couple of nights, I read your books to find out what goes on in that head of yours.

"I don't want to know if you have actually done any of those things. I choose to believe that you just have a very vivid and sexy imagination Mrs. McKnight. However, now I want you to make those sounds because I'm making you feel some kind of way. So don't be surprised if you wake up and I'm inside you or sucking something on you." He was looking at her body as he spoke. "And one other thing. I think we need to try out a couple of those sex scenes from your books as we christen the rooms in this house. What do you think?"

"I'm game" she responded, a little shocked. "But first tell me, where is that conservative guy you claimed to be? I'm expecting Mr. Missionary and you have been none of that. Not even close."

He smiled and said "We are married. I'm giving you everything I've got and eventually a few of my fantasies. I just wanted to see how you would respond to the prospect of a straight and maybe unimaginative man."

"So did I pass your test? I'm not sure if I should be upset that you were testing me or appreciate your approach to surprising me."

He nodded yes. "I saw you hesitate, trying to figure out if I was serious. Your face said you wanted me and whatever I had to give, so here we are. Are you disappointed? Would you rather have Mr. Missionary?"

She rubbed his butt saying, "there's nothing wrong with the missionary position. Glad to know there are options with you."

Their dinner was light and fast. They both wanted to

get back to bed. Robert was all Alpha male, with a laser focus on her satisfaction. He didn't need direction or affirmation. He was a very skilled lover. Whenever Pat tried to do any more than rub his back, he pushed her hands away and said, "Today is my day to get to know you and your body. Your desires. I live to please you now."

Making love every morning would become the best start to their days. They called it 'Morning Magic.' Both of them had very healthy sexual appetites.

On Monday, Pat scheduled the movers and Robert got the signed license off to Tommy on his way to work. Tommy called on Tuesday night to say that the license had been filed. Robert and Patricia were 'officially' husband and wife. They both beamed with joy at what God had brought together, pledging and believing that neither of them would feel alone or lonely ever again.

On Thursday they drove to Houston to pack and the moving company brought her life's belongings to Dallas early the following Tuesday. While Robert was at work, Pat put everything in place just as she had seen it in her head the first day she walked through the door, including moving out of 'her room' to recreate her bedroom from Houston with all of her furniture and artwork. She put her clothes and toiletries in the master bedroom and bath and her writing papers and books in the office. Her living room furniture went into the media room. New furniture pieces were delivered to fill in the remaining two empty bedrooms, and a handyman came to put up mirrors and pictures and light fixtures. By the end of the day, it looked like a full, lived in house. Even the handyman said he would love to live there.

When Robert came home from the gym, she met him in the garage and asked him to enter through the front door. He heard music playing as he walked in and smelled the eucalyptus. He moved through the house slowly, room by room, holding her hand and taking in the sights. His smile got bigger and bigger with each step. "This. Is. Home." he said in a low voice. "I love it and I love you. Thank you."

Robert asked Pat if she was ready for her Porsche Panamera. He had not forgotten. "We can order it so you would have it for your birthday. It would bring our transition full circle, both of us having our dreams come true."

Pat was pleased at the offer but declined. "I think I'm over my obsession for a Porsche. We have your Range Rover, the Audi, and the Lexus. That's enough. I have a great, full life with you and that is what I really needed. How about you just rent one for me for a weekend for my birthday?"

"Done," was Robert's only reply. "Wait. When is your birthday?" Robert was embarrassed when he realized that he did not know.

"November 10th." Their birthdays both being on the 10th (hers in November and his in May), made Robert smile. He liked that they had that in common. "Very cool," he nodded, already starting to plan what he would do for her.

CHAPTER NINETEEN

Robert asked Pat to plan to come to his office to meet his partners and staff. She hated the idea of being on 'display' but knew it had to happen sometime. Friday was the designated day.

The office was on the top floor in a typical corporate building but the security staff at the street level front desk had to get approval from someone in the office to let visitors up and they used a special key in the elevator to unlock the access to the floor. When she got off the elevator there was a wall of glass and the receptionist had to buzz her in. Everyone used their badges to move about from office to office or conference room.

The receptionist was a beautiful woman named Grace. About 5'9", she was well built and well dressed with nice mocha skin. Her hair and nails were done to perfection. She was the right 'face' for the company as the first person visitors see when they arrive. Grace had been there since it opened, first as a temp, then brought on permanently. She was curious about who this woman was since she had no information on an appointment for Robert. Robert had given permission directly to security for Pat to enter the floor when she came so Grace had not known of Pat until she was waiting to be buzzed in.

Pat was curious about whether Robert had ever dated Grace. Or wanted to.

As she waited for Grace to call Robert, a man came from one of the offices and asked Pat who she was and who she was there to see. Pat asked "Who are you and why do you need to know since the receptionist is doing a fine job of doing her job?" She turned back to look at the receptionist. Grace gave Pat a polite smile.

The man was standing behind Pat, looking her up and down, sizing her up when Robert came out. He told the guy, whose name turned out to be Frank, "you don't want that man, too much for you and besides she's not available."

"How do you know her? What is she doing here? Is she a new client?" he inquired.

Robert invited him back to his office and stopped along the way to get Howard, the other partner. Once everyone was together in Robert's office Pat took a moment to notice that they were three handsome, well-dressed Black men in their suits and ties. Very corporate and all about the business. It was the first time she saw how serious Robert was in a business environment. She was impressed. And proud.

Robert introduced Howard who, in addition to regular accounting projects, was responsible for staffing/human resources; and Frank, the nosey one from the reception area, had his own accounting assignments and took care of operations/office contracts/building services.

When Robert introduced Pat as his wife and told them that they were married the night they met, both Howard and Frank looked at Pat like they were looking at a ghost and said "D-A-M-N" at the same time. They believed Robert to be a confirmed bachelor, not even interested in marriage, and had never seen a woman at the office with him. And married on the first day? They kept looking from Pat to Robert, probably trying to figure out what she had or what she did to make that happen. They even speculated out loud about two women who worked there who would be devastated because rumor had it they both wanted to become Mrs. McKnight.

Thanks for the heads up, Pat thought.

The real reason Pat was there was to meet with Human Resources, then Robert's personal attorney to discuss and, as appropriate, sign paperwork: health and life insurance, power of attorney for healthcare and business along with the succession plan for the company, adding her name to investment and bank accounts, and papers to modify the title on the house and condo. She even got her own platinum AmEx card in her married name.

Now Pat fully understood why Shelly asked about a pre-nup on the first night. He was very well off and if they divorced, she stood to get a nice piece of money. Even his lawyer kept asking, "Are you sure you want to do all of this at once? We can wait."

Pat asked to have a moment with Robert so she could ask him the same question. He had set up a trust fund for TJ's college education and Shelly and TJs names were on everything else. She could live with that for a while, until they were both sure things were going to work out between them. But Robert was all in and this was his way of affirming that. And yes, Shelly knew what he was doing today. He assured Pat that he believed she would be fair if they split up so it was up to her to sign.

The pressure was phenomenal. Pat knew she was not ready to sign her mom's insurance and house money over to him so she tried to explain as tears formed in my eyes: "The money is all that I have left in the world of my family and what I could use to take care of myself if anything happened. I love you and believe all will be well, but I need to have some kind of safety net for myself. Just for a little while please."

He knew she had about three hundred thousand dollars, not nearly as much as he had or enough to live a big fabulous life. It was enough of a nest egg to keep her secure along with a steady job and selling some stories or books.

His response was to hug her and say, "Of course Pat, keep your money. I have enough for both of us. But I want you to sign these papers today. I want to know that you will be taken care of if something happens to me – either sickness or death. I would, however, like power of attorney over your healthcare so that I can make decisions that let me take care of you if you get sick. I don't want to have to wait for some of your family to get here from Houston."

That was more than fair. God was showing out once

again, giving Pat more than she ever asked for or needed. After all the papers were signed with the attorney, Robert escorted him out then came back to his office, locking the door before he sat down. He began pulling out more papers. Pat read the letterhead which said Federal Bureau of Investigation (FBI). Pat's antennae went up.

"What's this about?"

Robert became very serious and explained, "As my wife there are some things we need to discuss, things that are important for you to know and do as an agent's wife."

"The bureau has its own set of rules that you need to know and papers that you need to sign too. First, let me remind you that we never tell people that I am an agent. Not an uncle, an aunt, cousin, sister/friend, no one. Even Shelly, Tommy and I don't discuss it in front of TJ. When Shelly and I are talking about things related to the agency we never use the words Federal Bureau of Investigation or the FBI acronym. Can you do that? Not tell anyone? Not mention it?"

"Yes." Her mind was racing but he had her complete attention.

"Great. Now don't get mad, but I had to get your security clearance before today so I took your driver's license and credit cards one day and made copies. That's how I was able to cancel your car rental the day you were mad at me. Everything checked out. You're squeaky clean. All clear and a couple of the women at headquarters said they want to read your books."

"Okay. Why was the sneaking necessary? You couldn't just ask me?" She was frowning.

"Yes, but it would have raised a lot of questions that I couldn't answer until you were fully committed here."

"Okay. So what's the purpose?"

"They need to be able to verify your identity so they use a picture and your signature. We will also need to scan your face and body and take your fingerprints to put you in the security system for headquarters, here and at home."

"Okay" she said again. "What's next?" She could sense there was more than just signing papers and body scans.

Robert responded. "Once or twice a year I have to go to Quantico, Virginia or some other field office for a week on assignment. I never know when, they usually give us a couple of weeks' notice."

"And what do you do there for a week?"

"Usually work with the new recruits on shooting, get updates on software, maybe work on a project. I have to go as part of my commitment to keep my credentials and our assignments here in the office coming. Howard and Frank have to do it too. They try to have us go one at a time so the workload can be spread between two of us instead of one of us having to do the job of all three."

"Okay. Can I go with you?"

"No honey. We stay on campus and work long hours. No wives or families allowed. I can call you every day and we can video chat with each other. It will be like I've gone to a conference and will be home before you know it."

"What else Robert? What bomb are you about to drop?" She could feel the hairs stand up on the back of her neck.

"Well, there is also the possibility that I will be called out on a special assignment without much notice. So I have to always be ready."

"What kind of 'special assignment'?" She had an intense sense of dread.

"It's an assignment like going to Quantico, but different, more involved. Sometimes they are called missions. It could be anything, anywhere in the world. On top of the safe I keep a bag packed with clothes and toiletries that I'll need and there's room for the guns and ammunition I take."

Chills went down her spine and fear rose up in her throat.

"How often does that happen?"

"Not often since we started the company. Twice for me. Once for Howard and twice for Frank. When it happens, I'm off the grid for a while and you will be on your own until I come home. I can't contact you and the bureau will not give you any information. I'll just show up one day when the special assignment is over. So you can't have your boy toy at the house. I might be back at any time." He was trying to lighten the mood and be funny but it was not working.

"And you don't know how long you will be gone?"

"No baby. There is no way to know until I get on the road with the team. But once I know the details I still can't tell you. And I can't talk about it when I get back."

"Oh" was all she could say. She knew by the way he looked at her and talked that he meant dangerous, life and death.

"I promise you this though: if I am ever on a special

assignment and can get a message to you, I will. Someone will call you. They will tell you that they have a message for you. If they say who it's from they may say it's from The Hawk. Not Robert. Not Mac. Not McKnight. The Hawk. It is my nickname from training with my brothers. We all have one that just the five of us use. This is why I asked that we never go to bed angry, that we resolve our differences first. If I ever have to leave at the last minute there will be no time to talk things out. I don't want any regrets, for either of us."

Pat looked at him quietly for a while, memorizing every feature on his face, every hair follicle, the shape of his eyes and nose and ears and mouth. He sat quietly watching her watch him while she processed all of this.

Finally, she said "Okay. What else?"

"I know this is a lot, but you'll get used to it. Our lives will not really change from the way we've been living so far. But you need to know all of this. I am glad to finally be able to share it with you. And if we need to talk about any of this after you have had a chance to think about it, let me know. So we're good? You're still all in with me? Not running away?" His look was both afraid to ask and hopeful.

She responded quickly, "Yes, of course. I love you Robert. It's a bit much but I'll work through it. I'm good for now."

"Great! So now you need to sign these papers. The first one is designating you as the first point of contact instead of Shelly in case they need to communicate something about me."

She knew that 'something' meant missing, severely wounded, or dead.

"The next document appoints you as the power of attorney over my health care. I know you signed one earlier, but this is specifically for the bureau."

"The last one designates you as the beneficiary for my life insurance."

They filled in the blanks and signed each one, including a power of attorney for medical care for her. They were sitting on his sofa so he pulled her into his arms and held her for a long while. Then he took her to a room to scan her face and body and take her fingerprints, made copies of the paperwork for the safe at home, and finally prepared to send the originals to Quantico via FedEx.

"I wish I could have shared this with you before now but I couldn't. Thank you for being so understanding. I know you will worry when I am away, but trust me, I'll always be extra careful so I can get back home to you. I love you with everything that I am and everything I have.

"One final thing. This is personal. I have four best friends in the bureau. We all came through training together and had a few close calls early on in our careers. We have been there for each other in a lot of ways and will be brothers for life.

"Howard and Frank are two of those friends. Then there is Elliott and Dexter. Howard was the only married one. The other three are single and can be a bit out there. Fun and crazy. They are very serious about what we do but they are not as uptight as I am. They do more special assignments because they are single. I trust them with my life. If anything ever happens to me, I know they will be there for me as I will be for them, and at least one of them will watch over you on my behalf in case I'm not around.

"I want you to get to know them and hopefully you will trust them and grow to love them like they are your brothers too. Elliott and Dexter usually stay with me when they are in town. Sometimes for a day or two, sometimes for a week or more until they get another assignment. Once you have a chance to meet them I would like for you to tell me if you are comfortable with them staying with us. If not, it is no problem. They will go to Franks or somewhere else. You are my number one priority."

Pat did not respond verbally. She squeezed him tight, wishing she could crawl inside his arms and into his body and never come out.

When Robert and Pat walked out of Roberts's office, Grace asked them to go to the conference room. The partners had called the whole company together and wanted them there.

When Howard made the announcement that Robert was now a married man and Patricia was his wife, the guys whistled and called out playfully: 'Alright Mr. Mac' and 'No more Mac Man. Good. Less competition.'

Most of the women were smiling and clapping but Pat quickly figured out which two wanted him. Grace quickly walked out of the room after the announcement was made. For a brief moment she looked very disappointed but otherwise kept her composure. The other woman, Leslie, stayed in the room but had this evil look on her face, like she was not to be defeated.

Pat smiled and looked at Robert. He whispered, "Don't worry baby. There is nothing there for me. Neither one. Nothing. And anyway, I never mix my money with my personal life. In fact, co-owners can't do that here." Enough said.

After the staff left, Frank locked the conference room door and closed the drapes so that no one could see inside the room. He and Howard both hugged Pat and Frank said "Welcome to the family Sis. We really are happy that you finally tied this man down. He is a good guy and we thought he needed a wife, especially after his folks died so suddenly, but as time went on nothing happened so we thought he was a bachelor for life. It looks like he hit the jackpot with you. He has not stopped smiling today so he is very happy."

Howard added, "I hope he told you that if he needs anything, you just let us know. Now that goes for you too. I cannot wait to tell my wife Yvonne about you. She has been dying to have another wife in the group. I think you two will get along well."

Pat gave him her number and Yvonne called that night to set up lunch for the next day. The guys were going to be playing ball so Yvonne and Pat had plenty of time to get to know one another. Pat needed a friend in Dallas, especially one on the 'inside.'

CHAPTER TWENTY

Howard's wife, Yvonne, was the sister from another mother that Pat never knew she always needed. From Richmond, Virginia, she was raised by her dad and two brothers after her mom died when she was ten. She had a male sensibility and perspective, very no nonsense, very little sentimentality. She knew how to hold her own around men and took no prisoners when it came to male/female relationships.

Yvonne's Aunt Shirley, her mom's sister, stepped in to provide the feminine influence on hair, make-up, how to dress and act like a lady, and how to navigate relationships, especially when you got your heart broken which would inevitably happen.

Attractive and confident, Yvonne played basketball and ran track in high school and college so her body was toned and muscular with womanly curves. Yvonne majored in business management and marketing at Spelman which eventually led to her current position as a sales executive for a medical equipment company. It was in Atlanta while in school that she met Howard.

Howard was from Brooklyn, NY and definitely had that New York attitude, confidence, and swagger. He was a tall man, on the slender side but he had muscles.

He was quiet but fun, always had a snappy comment or question that came as a surprise to the people he was engaging with who had no clue about his personality.

He spotted Yvonne at a party one fall night early in the semester. She already had a date so he stood on the sidelines, watching her and listening to her as she talked to other people. He was used to getting his way with women but somehow he recognized that he had to have a different approach to impress Yvonne. He learned that she played basketball and ran track so he showed up at all of her games and meets that year. They dated off and on for several years. He eventually went to FBI training and on assignments; she graduated college and started working. She dated other people. He did too. Somehow, they always managed to reconnect with each other. During one of his special assignments, he decided he needed her as his wife without any further delay so when the assignment ended he asked and she said yes.

When Pat told Yvonne about how she met Robert and his proposal that same night, Yvonne high-fived Pat and said, "You must have been his kryptonite because I never saw him act like that with anyone else. I really like Robert. He is a brother to me like he is to Howard."

From that day on, they talked a couple of times a week and hung out whenever the men were together on Saturday. Yvonne said with the hours she worked, she didn't have a lot of time to find new friends and she really appreciated having one who could understand her total situation with Howard.

Now that they were officially married and Pat had

moved to Dallas, she wanted to see all of her Dallas family, not just phone calls and texts. Over Labor Day weekend, she invited them over to play cards and games. They knew that she was married because Aunt Ginny could keep nothing to herself. But they had no idea that she had actually moved to Dallas, something they had wanted since they had moved there several years ago.

They all came when she called. That was how they were. Family. Aunt Vera with Uncle Jackson and their sons Jason and Jack, Jr. plus Aunt Barbara and Uncle Aaron with the girls: Vicky (Victoria), Sheila, and CeCe (Cecilia). When they walked in and saw the artwork and table in the foyer they knew immediately that they were from the Harris family home and started dancing and hugging Pat. They were so happy that she had finally left Houston and was living close by that they weren't even mad that she had gotten married without any family present.

Her aunts had discussed Uncle Roy's interrogation so they didn't try that question and answer session again. They just spent time getting to know Robert as they ate and played bid whist and spades and danced. They all could see that there was something special between Robert and Pat by the way he looked at her and hugged or touched her whenever they were near each other. Aunt Vera even confirmed what Aunt Ginny had said, that Robert and Pat acted like Paula and Patrick did in high school and until he died, like there was no one else in the world but the two of them. That made Pat feel so good and a bit teary eyed. It felt like another affirmation that she had made the right decision.

CHAPTER TWENTY-ONE

For the rest of September they went back to their weekly routine and made their monthly visit to Houston. Pat was focused on writing while Robert was busy with organization and community meetings and preparing for tax season. One Thursday night she gave him the first couple of letters to read, from the novel she was writing, that Walter sent to Gloria. She reminded Robert that Walter is an English professor so he loves words in poetry and quotes and books, contemporary ones as well as those that are now classics, so he is using all of his language skills to communicate to Gloria in his own style. Robert pulled up a chair behind her at the desk and read over her shoulder.

> *"Dear Gloria-*
>
> *I am very glad to have met you and happy that I can now hear your voice on a regular basis. I find it and you very pleasing. I like the feeling I had when I first intruded on your presence at the conference and for both of the days we spent together. You have an energy that is palpable and very attractive. Our conversations were*

stimulating, full of life and hope, coupled with a tone of confidence and creativity.

You are beautiful and assertive and talented, a wonderful combination that I like. You have awakened an interest I would like to pursue. I don't know who you are, but I want to get to know you. I don't know what you want, but I am hopeful that I may be able to provide it. I don't know what you have been through, but I am confident we can share it and move on to create positive new experiences. I pledge to first seek in you the foundation of friendship, then ask that we dwell in possibilities of how to make our days together uplifted spiritually, intellectually, and emotionally, even when we are both faced with life's challenges. I hope that is of interest to you.

Be well and be at peace until the next time…
Walter"

Robert paused at the end, thinking about what he had just read. Then he said, "I like that. He really laid his thoughts out there. Putting them in a letter made him sound so romantic and heartfelt. Not like a man with a line. Women like that, huh? Letters? Cards too? I guess I better step up my game." Pat could feel his breath on her ear and her neck and her body became hot with sexy thoughts and anticipation. All she could think was that his game was just fine, but if he wanted to do more, she would be happy to see it.

Pat shared one more. She explains, "They have been talking and texting for a few weeks when they agree that he will visit her in the town where she teaches. This is his note to her after he returns home."

"Dearest Gloria-

Evening is approaching but I can't let the day end without expressing my thoughts to you.

I don't remember the plane ride home. I was lost in my feelings about being with you and being able to take our relationship beyond the hand held technology of today. Our time together was magnificent. Wondrous. You taught me a new definition of what a hug feels like; what a kiss full of spirit and womanly desire could taste like, how exploring your body redefined intimacy for me. Our talks gave me the gift of watching you become radiant as you shared information about yourself and your life, and introduced me to your family through photos and heartwarming stories. I saw a woman who was loved and loving, whose spirit is contagious and fresh. Seeing you in your own space out of bed was fun and educational as I watched you navigate the streets while driving us around and in the stores while shopping and the way you selected the restaurants then relished the food. Thank you for renewing in me a joy, a rebirth in my life that had become routine and commonplace. I am eager to continue to explore these feelings on the next call

and your visit here in thirty days. Until then, I
end this note with adoration and admiration.
   Walter"

Robert was quiet for about a minute then he turned her chair around to look in her face and rub her arms and hands. He thanked her for sharing her progress and the letters but was overwhelmed with the desire to kiss her so he leaned in and did so. Then he said, "I don't know if I can handle much more. I might have to wait until the book comes out. You are very talented, good with language and bringing emotions to life. This is so sexy and it's not the obvious stuff Shelly talks about in the books she reads. I just want to lay you on this floor and make love to you. She has got to marry him at the end, right?"

Pat laughed and thanked him for his kind words. She assured him that there was trouble further along in what she had written that needed to be resolved before she could decide on the ending. He was so proud of her, watching her heart and soul come to life on the pages. He gained a whole new respect for writers and his love for her went up a couple of notches. They went to bed and had Night Magic before falling asleep.

CHAPTER TWENTY-TWO

Pat and Robert continued their search for a church home, having visited several different Baptist churches, alternating their visits every other week or so then narrowing their decision down to two places they both liked. On the last Sunday of September, as they were leaving the church that was furthest away from home, Robert went to the men's room and Pat headed for the car.

Before she could get there, she was cut off in the path by none other than Eric Carter, her ex-husband, the man who taught her the meaning of not being enough for someone. He was as shocked to see her as she was to see him. She had nothing to say and kept trying to move around him. He held her arms to stop her. Pat pulled back from his touch and asked, "What do you want Eric?" hoping he could hear the disinterest in her voice and leave. No such luck.

He said, "Wow. I am so glad to finally see you. I always hoped that I would someday. You look fabulous Pat. I am here for my cousin Brian's wedding and I'm leaving tonight. Can we go somewhere and talk?"

"No, and you have sixty seconds to say what you want."

"I'm sorry. Really sorry for what I did. I never meant to hurt you. I was not a good person, very immature and definitely not the man you deserved. You were so good to me. I had never been loved like that before and I did not know what to do. I was stupid and did very stupid things. I just want you to know that."

Pat felt Robert walk up behind her before he even touched her and asked if she was ok. He had heard Eric's apology.

"I will be. This man has thirty seconds to say what he has to say then we can go."

"How about you introduce us?" Robert asked, curious because he could see that Pat's attitude had changed dramatically since they walked out of church and that she and the man clearly had a previous relationship.

"Sure. This is Eric Carter, my ex-husband."

Robert stepped to Pat's side and looked at her saying "Your ex-husband? I thought your husband was dead?"

Eric looked at Pat, shocked and sad.

Pat shrugged her shoulders. "He is to me," she responded, looking directly at Eric then her watch, reminding him of his last thirty seconds.

Eric asked Robert if he would just allow him a moment with Pat, they had unfinished business. Pat frowned, saying "No the hell we don't." Then looked at her watch again.

He started talking fast. "Ok Pat, just hear me out. Did Gwen call you?"

Gwen had been their financial advisor. Pat did not respond.

"I finally sold the house and just this week gave her the check for the proceeds. I didn't take any money out. You deserve it all, not just half."

"And would you please call my mom? I know I have no right to ask anything of you, but this isn't about me. I moved back in with her because she is having some serious health issues. She always asks about you. I know she would love to hear from you. Thanks for listening to me Pat. I am sorry. And I'm glad I had the chance to say that to you in person."

"Okay. Let's go Robert. We're done here." She wasn't bitter or angry. She was indifferent. Robert's love had made her feel so good that she could finally let go of the hurt Eric had caused.

He motioned for Eric to move and ushered Pat over to their car. She got in and turned her head to look out of the passenger side window. Robert started the car and turned the air on but did not move. "When are we going to talk about this? Now or at home?"

"At home."

Robert got them there in record time. Neither of them spoke. He grabbed a beer and sat at the kitchen island, waiting to hear what she had to say. Pat went to their bedroom to change clothes but first brought him a cell phone and some ear buds so he could play the video she had pulled up without her being able to hear it.

"Push play when you are ready." She walked back into their room and closed the door. When she knew Robert should have seen and heard it all, she came back out to ask him if he was ready to eat. He stared at her, following her every move with his eyes. When she walked over to him to get her phone, he pulled Pat into his arms and close to him. She looked in his eyes and asked if he had any questions.

He said, "I could have him killed for you." He would do anything to help her get over the pain of that experience.

She laughed and said, "No thanks. I need you here with me, not in prison. But thanks for the offer."

What he saw, and heard, was a video of Eric having sex with two women in a hotel. The camera was very close, as if they were making an X-rated movie. It started when the women entered the room nude and undressed him, pushing him back on the bed. First they had all possible positions of oral sex, then Eric invaded every orifice of their bodies, and relished in his ability to elicit sounds of real, almost surprised satisfaction from them both. It was his fantasy on film forever.

"How did you get this?" Robert was still watching her closely.

"Someone sent it to me. Maybe Eric by mistake. Or maybe on purpose. I don't know. I say God intervened, looking out for me.

"Eric had gone to Las Vegas for a fraternity conclave. That came on the second day he was away. By the time he came back from the trip at the end of the week I had quit my job, moved out of the house and on to Houston, and had a lawyer ready to serve him divorce papers.

"He called several times a day for a few days, trying to find me, so I sent him the video. I have not seen or talked to him since the day I got it. This is when I learned to compartmentalize. Otherwise I would have killed him."

Robert kept holding her and whispering, "I'm so sorry you had to go through this. I will never cheat on you. I promise. I swear. You didn't deserve that."

Pat smirked, saying, "I know I didn't deserve it. And you had better not. Truth? If this ever happens to me again, someone is going to die." She looked him in the eyes to let him know it would definitely be him and she meant every word. She didn't care about him being an agent or a marksman. He would be no match for the fury she would unleash on him.

With that conversation over they made dinner together and cuddled on the sofa in the family room. The television was on but neither one was watching. She didn't know what Robert was thinking but he kept looking at her. She finally turned the TV off and asked him if he now understood why she was so devastated with the Lynnette situation. To be clear, she gave him more information than he probably wanted to know.

"This wasn't the only time that Eric was unfaithful. Before he made this video, he had been cheating and leaving me without explanation for a night or a week-end. I stayed with him way too long believing that we could work it out but he wasn't interested. That's when I learned to cut my losses and why I didn't want to be with you after the baby business. I didn't want to be stupid and stay too long again. That's also when compartmentalizing became so important and necessary to me. And why I was — and still am sometimes — so terrified that you might be with someone else."

Robert said he understood completely and promised he would never make her feel that way. Pat also shared with him who Gwen was. "She was our financial advisor, and once I speak with her I want to add the proceeds from the house as well as my 'nest egg' to the family money. I'll have Gwen call you." Pat might not have Robert's level of money, but at least she had something decent to add to the family finances now and there was no need to keep things separate anymore.

He was happy to hear that. Not for the money because he didn't need it, they didn't need it. He was happy because it meant that Pat was 100% all in with him. The McKnight team was fully united.

And they agreed to go to the church closest to home to try to avoid any other encounters with ex's.

CHAPTER TWENTY-THREE

In October, Robert came home nervous and would not look Pat in the eye. When she asked what was wrong he said it was a new client and he was trying to fit the business into the schedule before tax season. Somehow, Pat knew better, but didn't press. She waited to see what was to come. Her dad had taught her to be patient when she was a kid because she always got so excited and restless, like for her birthday or Christmas.

The next night Robert came home anxious but again she waited. The next morning he got dressed and said the four words people dread hearing: "We need to talk." Pat cringed and tried to brace herself as she got out of bed and headed for the kitchen. She didn't want the stink of what was to come anywhere in their bedroom.

"Maxine Collins is the new client and an old friend from college. We spent a lot of time together during our college years. She got pregnant when we were both were seniors and had planned to get married. Before we made it down the aisle, she lost the baby. Soon after, we graduated and went our separate ways.

"It's been a few years since we have talked but she and her husband are having major tax problems that have also turned into marriage problems. She needed to know if she could go to jail for fraud or some other charges so she called me for help. She needed a high-level assessment to know what to do if the feds came after her. She is a schoolteacher and not involved in her husband's business, but she signed the tax papers every year so she wanted to know if that make her liable. Of course I said yes I would help. I would do it for any old friend." The way he talked about her, it was clear that he wanted to see her.

Pat wondered if their relationship had ended in grief and sadness over the baby and what might have been. They could even have unfinished business. The question was whether this time together was for permanent closure or for them to see that they were ready for an adult relationship.

Robert asked Frank to handle her case because she lived in Cleveland, Ohio and that was his area of expertise. When she came to the office to provide the details and paperwork for the case, she and Robert saw each other for the first time in years.

"We had lunch on both days she was in town, just catching up. She knows all the college friends you met so I gave her updates on everybody. The group never knew about the baby or plans to get married."

"Did you tell her that you were married?" Pat needed to know what story he told to bring Maxine up to date on his life. "Yes, of course," he responded, not sure of why that was even a question. He always wore his wedding ring.

"Has staying married now come into question since

Maxine has come back into your life?" He quickly answered, "No, why would you think that?"

"Just checking. You've been acting a little unusual this week, like you're nervous or hiding something." She needed him to know that he seemed different to her and hoped that he understood her concern. She didn't specifically call it out, but their morning sexual activity was different this week. Not as focused and playful. He was in a rush and couldn't look at her.

Pat started feeling like she had to fight for her husband so she told him quietly, "I love you, and I appreciate that you told me about Maxine." She was sad. Not even hurt or angry. Just sad that she was in this baby drama with Robert again. That seemed to be the price to pay when married to a handsome man. Pat knew she would not compete, even with such a strong college relationship and friendship that seemed not to have missed a beat after all these years.

"I'd like to meet her." It was a statement, not a question. Pat wanted to see for herself the dynamics of Robert and Maxine's interactions to decide what she should do. Robert hesitated for a moment then said, "Okay. Sure."

Maxine's next meeting with Frank was in two weeks for a deposition and to sign papers so Robert planned dinner for the three of them for that Friday night. Those two weeks were like two months to both Pat and Robert. Robert kept asking Pat if she was okay. Their morning sex was a little better, but he was still on edge and it showed.

When the day came, Pat made sure everything on her was right from head to toe—hair, make-up, and clothes. Everybody in the office seemed to know that Robert and Maxine were friends and had gone to lunch together during her last visit, just the two of them, not even with Frank who was handling her case, or with Pat.

Grace was looking at Pat with a smirk in her eyes, probably wondering if she knew the real deal between Robert and Maxine. Leslie had a smile on her face when Pat passed her in the hallway. She made sure to tell her that Robert was in his office with one of Frank's clients. She was enjoying what she hoped was going to be a big blow-up, thinking that Pat was about to meet a woman who wanted her husband.

Maxine was sitting in Robert's office when Pat arrived. Both Maxine and Robert were nervous, she was fidgeting with her watch. She kept looking at Robert for guidance on what to do. He greeted Pat at the door and gave her a hug and kiss as usual. Then he walked her over to where Maxine was sitting to introduce them. He was looking at Pat like he didn't know what to expect but he was braced for anything.

Pat stood by Robert and poured on the charm. "I am so happy to meet another of Robert's college friends. Robert has spoken highly of you. I'm sorry for your tax problems, but I know you're in good hands with these guys looking out for you. And thanks to both of you for allowing me to join the reunion." Maxine relaxed but Pat could tell that Robert was still tense.

Robert had chosen a nice restaurant for them to have

dinner so they talked for a few minutes about the type of food they served and how close it was to the office, then they all left together to walk over.

When they got to the restaurant, Pat asked her usual type of questions: "Tell me about yourself. How did you meet your husband? How did you get into teaching? How did you and Robert meet on campus? Just how nerdy was he?"

It was interesting to watch Maxine as she responded. She was an attractive woman and had a great life. She came from a large family and loved kids. After college she went back home to a teaching job, third grade. Her husband was the brother of one of her teacher friends. He had some kind of consulting business but she wasn't so sure now that it was the traditional management consulting like he had said, or if that was a cover for other things, things that led to the IRS investigation.

Her face became flushed and Pat could clearly see she was enjoying sharing her stories about Robert. "He was the typical geeky guy: quiet and always had a load of books in his arms around campus. We had a couple of classes together freshman year and shared notes and just started hanging out together at the library and parties. We went to Sunday church services together when he had to sing and I went to his choral concerts that were twice a year."

"So you were in love?" Pat had to ask.

Maxine looked at him. "Well to be honest, I was in love with him. He was actually my first love. But he never once said he loved me. I don't even remember him saying he liked me. We hung out together year after year; just comfortable together. And I kept some of the other girls from bothering him which, in hindsight was probably what he really wanted."

Pat looked at Robert and he looked at her but didn't say a word or show any emotion.

"And the baby?" Pat asked.

Maxine put her head down and sighed and said, "Yes, the baby. I always wanted children, but had no thoughts or plans to get pregnant in college. And we only had sex one time! Such a cliché. Robert was going to do the right thing but we both realized that getting married to each other would not have been good. We would have been divorced before long. So I believe it worked out for the best."

"And now?" Pat wanted to know if she had some feelings for Robert since their lunches.

She looked at Robert and said "He'll always be special as my first love, but that time has long past. I'm glad to see he's happy with you. I need to focus on my legal troubles, my marriage, and my family." She pulled out her wallet to show pictures. "I have two kids with my husband, both girls. They need me now more than ever."

Robert held Pat's hand under the table as he had done at restaurants since the day they met so she felt good about that. He kept looking at Maxine and Pat while they talked like he was at a tennis match, allowing Maxine to do most of the talking. When he saw that Pat was genuinely friendly, he relaxed a little, looked at her, and smiled.

The evening was winding down but Pat needed to make sure there was no reunion when Maxine got her life back together, especially if she and her husband didn't repair their relationship or her husband went to jail. Maxine went to the ladies room which gave Pat a chance to talk to Robert.

"So what's the real deal here?" she asked.

Robert looked at her with his head tilted to the side and a question in his eyes. He finally asked: "What are you talking about?"

"I can see that Maxine was probably a cute college girl because she has clearly grown into a delightful woman. So are you interested in going back in history and reclaiming your old relationship? Have you developed an interest in the adult Maxine since you've had these days of seeing each other? Do you want to wait for her to get her life straight and come back to you? If so, then you need to tell me tonight." Pat was nervous and talking too much and didn't stop to give him a chance to respond.

"Because I love you Robert McKnight. I have loved you since the day we met and I love you every day that we wake up together and every night when we go to sleep together. My heart beats for you. My cells regenerate so that I can live for you. I meant our vows 'till death do us part.' You need to let your past stay in your past. Stay with me — your present and your future. After tonight, no more reunions. No lunches or dinners or catch up or check in calls with old flames. Just me and you."

Maxine came back just as Pat finished talking so Robert never had a chance to answer. Pat prepared to go to the ladies room. She paused to say to them, "Well good people, I have enjoyed the dinner and the company, especially learning so much about my husband in his college days. But it is time to say goodnight. And goodbye. Goodbye Maxine. Safe travels back to Ohio."

With that, Pat got up and made her way to the ladies room. She loved Robert beyond reason and she needed him to keep loving her back. Did he choose her? She was about to find out.

When she opened the door to the ladies room she could see their table and it was empty, the busboys were clearing the dishes. She put her head down and inhaled deeply, praying to get past the tables and out the door before completely losing it. She turned the corner to head for the front door and there he was, leaning against the wall with his hand out like the day they met.

He pulled Pat into his arms and said "Of course I choose you. I chose you the day we met and I choose you every day with every breath I take. She didn't change that. No one will."

Pat hit him on his arm. "Then why did you act so funny when she started coming around? You were nervous, wouldn't look at me. Didn't tell me about your lunches. Even our morning lovemaking was different. You made me think I had something serious to worry about."

"Truth?" he asked. "Because I was afraid of how you would react when you found out that I was going to marry her and about the baby. I never knew how to tell you. There never seemed to be a good time, especially after what happened that night at the pool place with Lynnette and the son she claimed was mine. I knew there could not be another issue with a woman and a baby from my past to come up again or you would definitely leave me."

Pat did not confirm or deny.

Robert continued. "I never loved her Pat. We were good friends and the baby was strictly an accident. I didn't even ask her to marry me. I just said, 'I guess we have to get married then,' and she said 'Yeah, I guess.' Neither one of us really wanted that.

"I made sure that never happened again with any other woman. That's why I'm so adamant about using condoms. God knew you were in my future so he allowed me to grow up and get ready for you without having a child and ex-wife or baby mama drama. I'm grateful to Him for that."

"So tell me Robert, any other women coming out of your past with baby drama? I don't know if I can take another hit like this." She was glad that neither situation had resulted in a baby, but their luck might run out the third time. He was quick to assure her "No. Definitely not. Lynnette was a total surprise and now that you know about Maxine, I have no other surprises please believe me. After the Maxine fiasco, I have been super careful which is why I was confident that Lynnette was not telling the truth."

"So when do you want us to have children?" Pat knew they both wanted them but somehow in all of their talks timing had never come up. "Would you want to wait another year or two or five? Children change your life so we need to decide how long we want to wait."

He smiled. "I could see having a baby with you maybe in another few years after we have had some time together. I waited a long time for you. I'm selfish and want you all to myself a while longer. What about you?"

"I agree, not anytime soon. We've been through so much already and it hasn't even been a year yet! I can't imagine what else could come up but we need more time for just us before we bring another person into the mix."

"Okay." Robert was excited. "Then let's go home. I want to make love to you and hear you tell me again about how your cells regenerate just so you can live for me. That was super sexy when you said that. I have never heard anything like that before." Pat put her hand in his as they walked toward the door and said, "Oh, there's more where that came from Mr. McKnight. You make me want to say a whole lot of sexy things to you." It was Robert's turn to blush.

CHAPTER TWENTY-FOUR

In early November, they had another evening with his college friends, the first since the fiasco of the spring outing when Lynnette showed up, only this time it was at Jerome and Joann's home. They knew Robert would not be around again until after tax season so instead of a restaurant, they wanted a more personal space to play games, listen to music, and talk. Plus they had not heard anything about Pat so they wondered if Robert had managed to salvage their relationship. Pat was nervous about seeing everyone even though Robert had apologized on the Zoom call. He promised her that she had nothing to be embarrassed about, that his friends would be happy to see her.

When Joann opened the door and saw Pat, she smiled and hugged her, saying she was very happy to see her. Robert walked into the family room first and everyone was looking behind him to see if he had brought anyone with him. Roberts turned around to look behind him asking innocently, "What are you looking for?" He knew they were looking to see if he had a date. More specifically Pat.

When Pat and Joann walked in, the whole room erupted in cheers and shouts to Pat of 'welcome back.'

Robert smiled, reached for Pat, wrapped his arms around her and kissed her on her forehead. He whispered in her ear, "I told you to trust me. They are good people." She smiled her thanks at all of them.

The guys looked at him and each one started laughing and saying, "So how long did you have to beg CB? Did she make you suffer? What did you have to buy her? You were wrong man. Glad you got her back."

Jerome was the first to notice. "Do you guys see what I see? He is glowing like women usually do. Definitely in love. We have never seen you like this man. Ever."

"And he has teased every one of us about being whipped and having no control in our relationships. It's finally his turn to know how it feels to have real love in his life."

"Congratulations Ms. Pat. You are the one. Welcome to the family. We're all glad you two got past that first night we were together."

Robert could only shake his head and laugh. They teased him the rest of the night, especially when he called Pat to sit by him or when he held her hand. They were eager to remind him of some of the things he said to them as they fell in love.

"What's wrong with you man? Give her some space to breathe. You don't need to be all over her like that."

"Your nose is so wide open you are acting like you can't move without her."

"Make sure you get permission to go to the bathroom since you can't seem to make a decision without her."

They all loved Robert like a brother and had watched

his life evolve through the years. They were happy for him and for them, but still gave him grief.

Pat put her arms around him, kissed his lips, and announced to the group "Well I'm glad I'm the chosen one. I know he passed up a lot of ladies, some were questionable, if you know what I mean?" This was a nod to their previous restaurant experience. Pat continued, "There were also some great ones, probably including some in this room, so I feel special."

By the end of the night, Pat had a new group of sister friends. She didn't go to school with them, but she was definitely in the family now. They exchanged phone numbers and talked about getting together without the guys, maybe even starting their own book club, reading Pat's books first. It was a big boost of confidence for Pat that she and Robert were on solid ground and continuing on the path to their happily ever after.

CHAPTER TWENTY-FIVE

For her birthday, Robert took a week off, rented Pat a red Porsche Panamera, and surprised her with each step of the trip itinerary. First, they drove to Corsicana to visit a couple of wineries, then on to the *Magnolia Market,* spending the night at the luxury apartment hotel 1700 South 2nd in downtown Waco. Then on to Houston where he rented a suite at Hotel Zaza and held a sleepover party for Pat with Shelly and Pat's best friends in Houston, Laila and Yolanda and her cousin Gina; a girls night with lunch at the hotel and dinner at *Brennan's of Houston*, a Creole restaurant. They enjoyed wine from the wineries in Corsicana, balloons, flowers, and cake and ice cream, while Robert stayed with Tommy and TJ.

After the girls night Robert went back to the suite where he and Pat stayed for three nights before returning to Dallas. Her birthday present from him was a platinum choker necklace with their initials on the front on a heart shaped disc and the inscription "You are my life. Love, Robert" on the back. She was overwhelmed with love for him and the way he celebrated her. They christened every room in the suite with their Morning Magic, both very happy to be together.

CHAPTER TWENTY-SIX

Thanksgiving was fast approaching. Robert warned Pat that tax season was coming, and it was the most important part of his work. "It's my responsibility to complete year-end documents for the company and employees and our clients. I cannot afford any errors so I need a commitment from you that you will understand my long hours and fatigue. And please, we cannot fight during that time. I need to be focused and not have any turmoil in my life. That was part of the reason I never had many close relationships or got married. It was just easier to get through tax season alone."

Pat promised. She had been in corporate America for a few years and had publishing deadlines so she knew what it was like to be super busy and need to focus with no distractions. She could keep myself occupied and not be a bother.

"However," she said anxiously, "you know my issues with cheating and abandonment, so please do just two things for me: first, when you come home at night, no matter how tired, give me a quick hug and a kiss on the lips. It will take just a moment to acknowledge me and let me feel your presence. I need that to know that we are still connected.

"And the second thing is that sometime on Sunday I want two real hours with you. We don't have to go anywhere or do anything but be together and catch up, watch television, listen to music...I don't care. I just need to have some time with you."

He thought those requests were fair and gave his promise. The start date was the Monday after Thanksgiving and the end date was May first.

He also said they would do something special to celebrate after tax season and he would surprise her. That would be his first annual post tax season gift in appreciation for her support.

They spent Thanksgiving in Houston, staying with Shelly and Tommy. Everyone pitched in to cook, set up tables, and prepare serving dishes. They had invited family and people from the church who had no family in town for dinner, about twenty five or thirty at final count.

It was nice to meet more of Robert's family. His dad's two sisters, Georgia and Christine, were beautiful women who dressed very jazzy, and loved to dance and have fun. They each had a son, Kevin and Alexander respectively, so Robert and Shelly grew up with them, more like brothers than cousins. The boys were all big guys with broad shoulders and tight bodies from playing sports.

When they all descended upon the household, the chaos started. The young men were still unmarried and reminded Robert that they had a pact, to be each other's best men, so what happened? Robert could only smile and say he was sorry, but he had to act fast and couldn't let Pat get away.

They all told stories, the sisters of their latest travels and dates, and the young men talked about work and women. Finally, they got around to asking Pat questions about where she was from and what kind of work kept her busy and what she did to finally hook their nephew/brother-cousin. She gave them her standard answer "I'm a writer, born and raised in Chicago but most recently lived in Houston. And I didn't do anything to get Robert. God is good to me and Robert is my best blessing ever."

They said they were glad to see him so happy and knew that Robert's dad would approve.

Shelly and Robert looked just like their mother and her three brothers: tall, dark hair and lots of it, and warm brown skin color. They were all married. Wesley was quiet and watchful like Robert, Marshall was loud and liked to tell jokes, and Calvin made sure, when the church folks came, that everybody met everybody and felt comfortable, at home.

They all were happy for Robert and Pat too. Uncle Wesley shared with them that Robert's mother, Savannah had been worried that Robert would never settle down and get married and she felt he needed a good woman. He watched Pat throughout the day and before leaving told Robert and Pat that he saw a lot of Robert's mother in Pat, in the way she treated people and how she joined in the conversations so he was satisfied that Robert was in good hands. He said he believed Savannah would be pleased and maybe now could rest in peace.

It was Robert's turn to get misty eyed and he hugged Pat, kissing her forehead and saying, "I told you and Uncle Roy that you reminded me of my mom. See, I'm not the only one who thinks so."

It was a full and fun day and Pat went to bed very happy to be a McKnight.

On Friday, they stopped by Uncle Roy and Aunt Ginny's to hear the stories of their turkey day. They understood that Pat had to be with Robert's family for the first Thanksgiving and did not put any pressure on them to spend time with her family next year. They just wanted Pat to be happy and spend Thanksgiving with family, even if it wasn't them.

They went back to Dallas on Saturday after his day with TJ so that Robert would be home all day on Sunday and start tax season on Monday ready, not rushing.

CHAPTER TWENTY-SEVEN

The first month of tax season was like any other month. Robert mostly kept regular hours but repeatedly said it would be different in the New Year.

For their first Christmas Pat decorated the house but they agreed no gifts. They both had a lot of clothes and shoes and jewelry. The house was fully furnished. They didn't need another material thing. They spent the holidays in bed, choosing a different sensual experience from Pat's novellas to try. She picked the first one for Christmas Eve.

They went to the guest bedroom with the queen-sized bed. Robert was so used to being in control it was hard for him to relax. Pat started things off with a shower where she used a loofah to get his nerve cells at attention, then dried him off.

She had created a special playlist of romantic music to set the mood and carry them from foreplay all the way through to the end of the evening. A man she dated once told her that the right music can do a lot of the work for you in a romantic situation. She was about to find out and had about 45 minutes to get it done.

The First Time Ever I Saw Your Face by
Roberta Flack
At Last by Etta James
In You by Glenn Jones
You by Jesse Powell
Between the Sheets by Four Play featuring
Chaka Khan
Feel the Fire by Peabo Bryson
Together Tonight by Brian Culbertson
Sensuality by Brian Culbertson
Loves Serenade by Ramsey Lewis

She put ear buds in Robert's ear then turned the sound on low, asking him to focus on the music. That was her first step in taking command of some of his senses, so some would be heightened and others would decrease.

He had never had a massage so he laid on his stomach while she slowly rubbed his neck, his shoulders and arms, his back and legs and butt with warm massage oil until he was totally relaxed.

She rolled him over onto his back and stretched his arms out, handcuffing one arm to each side of the headboard, then tied a silk scarf around his face to cover his eyes.

Straddling his body she started by kissing him in the mouth for a long time, then doing to him what he had been doing to her for the past few months—licking and kissing and sucking his face and arms and hands and nipples, then going down one leg, and up the other leg, stopping center stage to open his legs wide, kiss his thighs, and lick him like an ice cream cone, long hard strokes with her tongue, and using her hands for pressure where her tongue had been until finally she locked her mouth around his tip. He was moaning and twisting and panting, calling her name over and over again and saying how much he loved her, how good this felt, and how this was his best Christmas ever.

With just a few soft sucks and a gentle pull, his body was pulsating, raising up off the bed and he let out a growl and a yell that came from deep in his throat. She had never heard that from him before. He moaned when she went to the bathroom for towels to wash and dry him off then, starting at his feet, massaged him all over the front of his body again.

When she got to his hands she unlocked the handcuffs and he took off the blindfold. He didn't open his eyes or say a word, just reached for her and held her very close and very tight.

Pat whispered, "I love you." He just nodded, and then drifted off into a deep, deep sleep.

When she woke up the next morning, he was staring at her and finally said "Good morning Sunshine." His voice was hoarse.

"Good morning handsome husband of mine. Merry first Christmas! Ready for breakfast?"

"Not yet. I need a minute."

"Are you okay?"

"Yes. I just need to come down to earth. Don't take this the wrong way please, but no one, not even all the women combined that I've ever been with has done all of that to me. You are AMAZING. I love you. So much."

"Awww. I love you too! Glad you liked it." Pat couldn't help but smile. It felt good to know that she did something to him and for him that no other woman had done. She hoped he remembered that in the days and weeks to come during tax season.

He cleared his throat and said softly "It was wonderful. It was everything. You are frisky and sassy and all kinds of sexy. And all mine. Merry Christmas to me."

For New Year's Eve they went to an adult store for a few items to use to christen the family room. They were both pleasantly surprised at the improvement in the quality of both the videos and the toys.

On New Year's Day as Robert watched the professional football game, they played their own 'touch football' game at the same time. Between the feathers and fur mitts and vibrators and massage oil, he was able to enjoy the game but also was distracted enough to anticipate what was about to happen.

For the first half of the football game Pat was his personal cheerleader. Robert really liked the easy access of the open front bras that she wore on the first day they made love so he had asked if she would only wear that style from that day on. Pat was more than happy to oblige.

For the game she wore a sheer white bra with lace trim and a matching thong underneath one of his white shirts, with only the center button keeping the shirt closed.

He just had on a t-shirt and pajama bottoms.

They made a bed on the floor with a thick comforter and a couple of pillows.

They chose sides so whenever either team made a touchdown, one of them had to remove an article of clothing and the other one got to use a toy on the body part that was exposed, and kiss and lick wherever they were so inclined. They got to play with each other until the next touchdown.

Robert's team was the first to score so Pat took off the shirt, leaving her bra and thong. He asked her to stand in front of the television with her legs wide open so he could watch the game between her legs while he used a feather to tickle her legs on the inside and outside and use the tip of the feather to rub across the sheer fabric of her thong in between her legs. He was slow in his movements and looked more in her eyes than at the game. It was erotic, mesmerizing.

When her team scored, she took his t-shirt off of him and dropped to her knees to give her full attention to his chest. She put on the fur mitts and, knowing his nipples were very sensitive, sucked on each one gently, as if he was feeding her her last meal while rubbing his arms and shoulders with the mitts. When she moved from his nipples, she alternately kissed and bit his shoulders and licked down to his navel and back to his nipples.

By half time, they were both nude. They put on a triple x-rated video and watched for a while, then started it from the beginning and did whatever they did. The sounds the actors were making were erotic and added to their excitement. When the winning team made the last touchdown, they had 'touched down' too.

The next day he got the call to report to Quantico, Virginia in one week. He was not happy to go just as tax season was starting but he had no choice. The upside was that when he got back he could be focused and not get interrupted again.

As promised, they talked on the phone every day and did video chat like he had a regular corporate job and was away at a conference or series of client meetings. They even tried phone sex a couple of nights. They decided they liked the talking dirty to each other part, but not when you hang up and you are all alone so they agreed to save that for when they were together.

He got back, tired, on Saturday evening so he had only one day to rest before he got deep into work. She gave him a regular full body massage with warm oils to help him relax.

CHAPTER TWENTY-EIGHT

As the weeks passed she could see that he had really long days and six day work weeks and it was getting harder to get a hug and kiss and claim her two hours of time on Sunday. He didn't even acknowledge Valentine's Day even though she was nude and dressed in a red ribbon when he came home. He had that distant look on his face like that night with Lynnette so he really didn't see her.

In late February, she noticed that he was coming home late and going straight to the shower and to bed. Barely a nod in her direction during the week and he slept all day on Sundays. She didn't fuss, but she mentioned one Friday "I haven't had a hug or kiss all week. Do you have one for me tonight?" He gave her a swipe on the lips and walked off. Didn't look her in the eye, no hug.

On Sunday, she stood in the doorway of the family room and asked if he had a few minutes for her. He was agitated. "What do you want?" he growled.

"Just to sit with you for a few minutes?" she asked. He never answered. She went over to sit by him on the couch and he fell asleep.

True to her word she didn't fuss. When he came

home, no matter what time, she was standing in the kitchen or family room so he couldn't help but see her. She wanted to make it easy for him to acknowledge her with a hug or a kiss. Something. At first he would look at her and nod but go straight to the shower and bed. After a couple of weeks he even stopped seeing her and nodding.

She always had food ready in case he was hungry. He never was. She left text and voice messages on his phone, saying "I love you" or "I miss you" and "Have a fabulous day" but he never responded. She sent him flowers but he never acknowledged them. She tried to shower with him at night but he walked out as soon as she got in.

Shelly shared her 7Up cake recipe so she could surprise him at work with a cake hot from the oven. He was in a meeting so she had to leave it on his desk with a note. He didn't even say thanks. Nothing seemed to work. He even stopped calling during the day to check on her.

Yvonne was her sounding board. She knew exactly what was going on at the office so she could help her think through what she should do.

Yvonne said, "Please don't do like I did. I almost cheated on Howard while I was away on business a couple of times our first year, with an old but still smoldering flame. We spent a couple of evenings together in hotels, drinking and talking. I did not sleep with him but came close. I soon realized that it was not right. Howard was the man I wanted so I never did it again. I don't think he ever found out but I feel guilty every time I think about it."

She pressed Pat. "It's the end of February. Can't you hang on for a couple more months?"

Pat confided in her about her first husband. "I've been here before Yvonne. I tried to be all that he said he wanted. I kept up my appearance, stayed on top of current events so I could hold my own with him and his corporate clients, and I tried to be sexy for him, initiating sex as well as being open to trying new positions. He stopped paying me any attention despite all of that. We worked for the same law firm and I knew his schedule but he would still come home late or not at all and acted like I wasn't there. I couldn't ask where he had been. He didn't talk to me except at work where he was polite enough to get through the day.

"He made sure I clearly understood that I was not who he wanted after all, that I was not enough. I believed that for too long then one day I realized he was a liar and a cheat and I deserved better. Why do women do that all the time—blame themselves instead of seeing the man for who he really is? I think I need to cut my losses early this time and not wait. I need to prepare to leave."

Yvonne thought that was a hasty decision so she asked, "What can we do to keep you occupied? Shop? Travel? Take a class? At least wait until tax season is over to give him a chance to present his side of the story."

Pat's best girlfriends in Chicago, Sherry and Linda, knew what happened with Eric and agreed with her that she should probably leave sooner rather than later.

Her Houston friends, Laila and Yolanda, didn't know about her history so, like Yvonne, they recommended that she wait until the end of tax season and get Robert's side of the story.

She already knew that waiting was not going to work. She didn't need anything so shopping seemed stupid. And she couldn't shop six days a week! She didn't want to travel without him. In fact, she was afraid to leave for a girlfriend trip for fear that if he didn't see her at all for a few days he would really forget about her. There was no class she wanted to take, no hobby to start, and she had been hired to teach but not until fall. She even stopped writing. Her mind would not focus. She was feeling alone and lonely already. Two more months of this, she thought, 'and I might be like my mom, in a never-ending depression.' She did not want that.

She finally opened up to Shelly who said she was disappointed in Robert, saying that she had asked him about her and how they were faring and he always said they were good. That hurt. He was talking to his sister during tax season but not his wife. And they weren't 'good' from her perspective so she didn't know why he told Shelly that.

Shelly asked her to please be patient, and shared how it was easy for her mother when their dad was on assignment for long periods because she had two kids to manage, a house to run and a full time job. Since Pat didn't have all of that, she asked her to hang on until May first. Just get through this first year and then talk to Robert.

Pat was back to square one. No one had a suggestion on how to get Robert's attention NOW so they could reconnect then he could finish the season.

She read an article that said one good way to keep from being bored, lonely, or depressed was to stop focusing on yourself and help someone else. For a couple of weeks she volunteered at the local food bank, packing and distributing bags of food, helping to stock the shelves of all the food that was donated by companies, and writing letters to companies to either ask for donations or thank them for their generosity for previous donations. Most of it was good physical labor that helped get her mind off her relationship issues.

Pat finally started back writing, but in the mornings instead of the afternoons, then going to the gym later in the day, stopping by a restaurant/bar called FEAST afterwards. It was in the mall, not far from the gym, and became part of her new routine. She was comfortable in restaurant/bars as a place she could go alone and have a drink and relax. She always sat at the bar and became friendly with the bartenders. At FEAST she quickly figured out her favorites to order in food (salad or chicken wings) and drink (a Moscato or Riesling or two), no more than two so she could drive home. She stayed until nine or ten p.m., looking at television and watching the patrons come and go, or she stayed until the basketball game was over.

Robert never got home before ten so he was not missing her. She just needed to be out of the house and around happy, engaging people.

What was odd was that whenever she tried to pay for her food and drinks the wait staff or bartender would not take her money. Not even for the tips. They always said the same thing: "Your money is no good here."

When she asked who was paying for it, no one could tell her. They just said they couldn't take her money and to order anything she wanted. Pat became nervous about that and debated on whether she should ask for the manager or just stop coming in. Nothing is free, and somehow she knew the price to be paid would eventually be more than the value of whatever she had ordered.

The same man and woman were always sitting at the end of the bar or at a nearby table many nights when Pat came in. She assumed they were a married couple, probably empty nesters who lived in the area and just stopped by to have dinner and drinks. They always nodded hello in that friendly way you do when you don't know people but you see them all the time.

After about three weeks their curiosity got the best of them and they finally came over and introduced themselves. Both were retired police detectives who worked for the owner, Joe Hunt. Joe was also a retired detective and paid them to be around so that he wasn't robbed, to stop fights, and to help drunk patrons get home safely.

Samuel Brookes was a big man with a little beer belly but still light on his feet and able to move quickly. He had a couple of adult children: a daughter lived in California, a son in New York. His wife died of a brain aneurysm the year he retired so FEAST gave him something to do. He was there every day.

Cynthia Willis was divorced and lived with her two

German Shepherds, retired police dogs. They were her kids. She had a friendly, fun personality but would turn lethal if you were out of order and didn't do what she said. She got her time in on the force and decided to get off street duty before something happened to her. She was promoted to the police academy, teaching new recruits. She came to FEAST from Wednesday through Saturday evenings.

They were protective of Pat and made sure she didn't drink too much and got safely to her car. They could see she was sad but didn't pry. Neither one would tell her who was paying for the food and drinks but told her not to worry, the truth always comes out, just wait.

Pat told them she was a writer so they regaled her with their war stories, cases they had covered while on the job and stories of people they encountered in FEAST. So many of their stories sounded like the many police dramas on TV these days. It's like what people say "Art imitates life."

They said they learned early on that you can't judge people by how they look or what they say. Some of the nicest, most affluent were also the meanest and had awful, bone chilling secrets. They also said they never got used to the rapes and murders and any case involving children. And each had to learn how to de-stress before they interacted with their families. It was somewhat common on the force to keep that anger bottled up inside at work then explode on loved ones.

Brookes and Willis had great imaginations too, and would make up stories about people who came in, especially couples, based on how they read their non-verbal communication. They had taken classes on Kinesics, the study of body language, at the academy, so they could describe what was happening between two people based on how close they stood together, how they were moving their heads (or not), their hand and arm position and signals. They also listened for laughter that was too loud or arguments that disturbed others.

While many couples who came into FEAST were on first dates or were couples having date night, sometimes people came out to eat thinking a public place would be neutral. Not always so. They told of a couple who were obviously not speaking when they came in, then he stayed on his cell phone so she reached over and stabbed him with a steak knife.

Brookes and Willis both said Pat was welcome to write about anything they told her, especially since they did not use people's names.

The three of them bonded quickly and formed their own little trio. Pat started sitting with them and even saw them in action a couple of times as people got loud.

CHAPTER TWENTY-NINE

One Thursday Pat walked into FEAST during happy hour and found all the bar seats full of women, a bit different from the usual clientele of a few men so she was curious as to why. As she walked toward Brookes and Willis, Pat saw for herself.

He was the new bartender. Tall, caramel color like her but with gray/blue eyes, a strong square jaw line, a beautiful smile, and a lean body that clearly went to the gym regularly because you could see muscles rippling under his short-sleeved shirt. Very striking and sexy as hell.

When Pat saw him, he looked at her at the same time. He was shaking a drink but stopped midair. The look between them was electric and unnerving. It was as if time stood still for a few seconds. Then the noise of the bar resumed and she walked to her seat at the table.

The women were trying hard to get his attention. Willis called it the 'pussy parade.' The bartender was using his charm and smiles and talking slick to them all as he poured drinks and raked in the money. It went on for over two hours until the evening bartender came in.

After coming from behind the bar, the new bartender

came directly to the table where Brookes and Willis were sitting so Pat thought he wanted to be paid for her order. She put her hand out with money in it but he pushed her hand back, looked at her for a few seconds then said the same thing the others had said: "Your money is no good here."

Turns out he was not the 'new bartender.' He was Mike Malone, the owner's nephew, and the co-owner and day-to-day manager of FEAST. He clearly liked and respected Brookes and Willis so he sat at the table and talked about the activity at the bar and when Joe was coming back from his extended vacation. The whole time he talked to them he looked at Pat and smiled.

She saw a man who was very handsome, self-assured, and probably dangerous. The kind who would hurt you, physically or emotionally, without a thought, if you crossed him. And who would make a woman a sex slave with his passion, doing all manner of wicked things to her.

Pat was glad she was married even though they were having very bad times. If she had been single, she could see herself surrendering to his charms and enjoying more than one decadent night with him.

When she was leaving he walked her to her car, asking what brought her into the bar every week. "How do you know that I come every week? I've never seen you here before." She was surprised

He responded, "I've been watching you on the security cameras. I think you are beautiful and have a smile that lights up my world. Brookes and Willis are suspicious of everybody but they love you. Now I know why."

"So are you the one paying for my food and drinks each week?" Pat inquired. He smiled and asked, "Do you mind? I want to take care of you."

"I'm married. I have a man to do that," she snapped.

"I've heard," he said, nodding. "But it looks like there might be trouble in paradise. I just want to be your safety net…if you ever need one."

"So this is your thing, preying on vulnerable women in troubled relationships?" Pat asked with attitude.

"No, I don't need to do that," he replied in a very serious tone.

"Then what do you want with me? You clearly have your hands full with what I saw at the bar tonight so I would never want to invade that life or compete."

He leaned in close and whispered quietly in her ear, "I want you to invade my life. All of it. Anytime. And I don't cheat so there would never be anyone for you to compete with."

"Such a charmer" she responded. "Goodnight Mr. Malone."

"Good night Lush," he replied, which gave her pause.

"What? Lush? If you've been watching me in the security cameras you know that I don't drink a lot. Why would you call me a lush?" she asked, curious but still with attitude.

His response was unexpected: "It's not about your drinking. I think you are luscious—to look at and now to talk to. Your voice is soft and sexy. And your eyes are soulful. You look at me as if you want to see me. All of me. I like that. Most people don't or can't look at you like that, probably because they are so self-absorbed. I want to look at you watching me do things to you. And who knows, if I'm lucky, someday you will. So that's my name for you Patricia McKnight. Lush. Drive safely. I can't wait to see you again." He closed her door and watched her drive away.

Beads of sweat covered her forehead. What a night she thought all the way home. And what a man. Really glad I'm married and I love my husband.

The next time Pat visited FEAST, Mike came out and sat with her and Willis and Brookes, expanding the trio to a regular foursome. It was nice to get to know him. He was fun and funny but all business when it came to FEAST. And Pat. He still refused to take any money from her and she didn't protest. Was she cheating on Robert?

Robert never noticed that Pat wasn't home when he got in. He probably thought she was in the office writing because she started keeping the door closed all the time. One night she went to their bedroom to see if he was still awake but he was not, and was spread eagled all across the bed, leaving no room for her anyway.

A deep familiar loneliness and hurt engulfed her and sat in her chest like a weight. She was devastated, depressed, and angry with herself again for falling for him. In her mind, this is why you need to just date someone for four seasons or some extended amount of time to get to know them. And whatever you do, don't live with them too soon.

Pat pounded the treadmill and took Zumba classes until she was exhausted, losing about 20 pounds in two weeks. The loss was noticeable. Brookes and Willis were worried but didn't say anything. They just made sure she ate full meals and only let her have one drink.

One night Mike asked her to come to his office with him. He closed the door and told her he couldn't stand watching her be sad and wanted to know what the hell was going on. "Is your husband hitting you?" he asked.

"No, of course not." Pat replied indignantly.

"Then what's going on? You have lost too much weight and you don't smile anymore. Tell me the truth. All of it. Or I'll have Brookes and Willis track him down so I can ask him."

Pat knew he would do just that so she shared the humiliating details of her husband who no longer paid attention to her in less than one year of marriage, and how he said it was going to be rough during tax season but she was beginning to feel like it was more than that. He could hear the anxiety and sadness in her voice.

Mike didn't comment on her situation, but offered "if you ever need a place to stay, I have a guest room that will always be open for you." Pat knew that could be dangerous. They were good friends, but she knew it probably wouldn't take much for them to cross the line.

As if he was thinking of the danger too, he said "I care too much for you to interfere with your marriage or try to take advantage of you. You need to make the right decisions about that. I'm just offering a quiet place for you to figure things out. I'm usually asleep when I'm home so you wouldn't have to worry about me knocking on your door."

Pat stopped taking Shelly's calls and only sent text messages to her family so they would not hear the anxiety and sadness in her voice. They would know immediately that something was wrong and she didn't want them to know just yet how stupid she felt though she knew they would be understanding.

She decided she wanted to move back to Houston and consulted a divorce attorney who drew up papers asking only for Pat's family money back and enough from Robert so Pat could pay cash for a nice but modest house in a good community and have money in the bank for taxes and upkeep for about twenty years. They estimated everything to be about a million dollars total, still leaving him with most of his fortune. Pat thought that was fair. The attorney wanted to push for more given his net worth but Pat only wanted what she needed to move forward with her life.

Staying in the house and being ignored was getting harder and harder to bear. She just cried all day thinking of how in the world she could manage another loss. So she decided to find a place to stay until May first and Robert signed the divorce papers. It was already April so there wasn't much time left. But she couldn't be in his house and not feel his love another day. Pat thought about her options.

Stay with Yvonne and Howard? They were both gone from home a lot, but Howard was Robert's friend. She had asked Yvonne not to say anything to him but couldn't be sure that Yvonne had honored her request. She did not want to get Howard or Yvonne mixed up in their mess, especially since she needed to stay more than a couple of days.

Stay with family? They didn't need to know how bad things were yet, not until she could get the divorce papers signed and start to move back to Houston. She couldn't stand to see their pity and hear them talk about divorce #2 and how she should not have been with him so soon anyway. She was not ready for them to rub salt into these open wounds.

Go to a hotel? Not a good place for a miserable single woman. She was already lonely and feeling unloved and depressed. She needed to be around somebody who cared about her, not be by herself.

Stay with Willis? Can't. Allergic to her dogs.

Stay with Brookes? He now lived in the RV full time so there was not enough room.

That left Mike's offer. She knew she would have her own space, he would make sure there was food that she didn't have to cook, and he was gone most of the time. And it was free with no judgement.

Pat moved in with Mike the last week of April. She still went back to Roberts's house and made sure it was clean, his clothes were ready, and there was beer in the fridge. She had to keep her promise until the very end of tax season. Robert didn't even notice that her car was not in the garage that week. At least he didn't reach out to say anything to her or even leave a note.

On her first night at his house, after FEAST closed,

Mike finally shared his life story with her. "I grew up with a single mother and three sisters in co-op city in the Bronx. It was rent controlled so we just stayed in my grandparents' apartment after they died. People used to do it all the time. My mom worked as a cashier in retail stores so there was never enough money.

"Uncle Joe never married or had kids so he was more like a Dad than an uncle. He helped us out here and there, but I became the primary breadwinner in the house when I was ten. Selling drugs, robbery, car theft. When I was fifteen I was arrested when I beat up my mom's boyfriend for beating her and trying to touch one of my sisters. I did a year in the juvenile detention center and got into a couple of fights with guys trying to use me to show everybody how tough they were.

"My mom's boyfriend was found dead and they questioned me about it, but since I was already locked up they couldn't pin it on me. Between that and the fights in the center, I got a reputation for being hard and mean even though I never started anything with anyone unless they came after me or my family.

"I got a girl pregnant when I was nineteen so we got married. We broke up after a couple of years because I never could get a regular job that paid any real money and she couldn't handle the other stuff I had to do to help us survive. I have a twenty year old son who is in college. He often stays with me during his school breaks and sometimes in the summer."

"Uncle Joe sent for me to come work for him so I wouldn't end up in prison. I've done everything in the place from sweeping floors and washing dishes to waiting tables and cooking. I even went to school to be a bartender, and I've taken classes on hospitality management and accounting. Yvette, my ex, didn't want to move to Texas so we both moved on with our lives. She eventually remarried and is happy and has another son.

"For a long time I lived off my tips and used my salary to buy my mom a house and pay the taxes and keep it up. Now that all of my sisters are grown and live on their own, I still send mom money to make sure she has enough to pay all of the bills and enjoy life. I bought in to the bar and the plan is that when Uncle Joe retires he will get a regular retirement check but I will be the sole owner. I stay busy with work and going to the gym and making sure my son is ok. I have my share of women but no one close or regular. Don't have a lot of friends outside of the business. I'm pretty happy. Except now I want you so that makes me uncomfortable since you're married."

Pat looked directly at him the whole time he spoke. His voice inflections, facial changes, and body movements all said that he wanted Pat to know all about him and believe that he was really a good guy.

When he finished he looked at her and smiled. "Hey Lush. You know I've never told anyone that much about me. This feels like a confession. I need a drink." He jumped up from the sofa and went into the kitchen, keeping his back to her. He needed a moment.

He clearly was not used to being so close and personal with anyone. Pat was glad to be the chosen one and felt like she wanted to hug him, but knew better.

CHAPTER THIRTY

On the morning of May first Pat was supposed to go to the company wrap party but she left divorce papers on the kitchen counter instead with a note:

My dearly beloved Robert:

A year ago you walked into my life and changed it forever. I was a broken soul, hurting, and frightened of you and the power I felt from you, the power to consume me. You gave me hope and the love I had been longing for. You made me whole again and I gladly gave you my heart, my soul, my all.

Unfortunately over the last twelve weeks my biggest fears have resurfaced and come true. I realize that I'm not enough for you. My love is not enough. It is secondary to work and maybe someone else too.

I heard your warnings about tax season and thought I was prepared, strong on my own but also fortified by your one of a kind love that made me take the leap of faith with you.

But tax season is a force to be reckoned with,

an unusual but effective mistress. She demands all of your attention, leaving no room for me for months at a time. I can't live with you and not be able to touch you or be held by you for so long. I need you and I can't compete. So I'm taking back my heart and giving you the space you need to be the best at what you do and not have a needy, lonely wife to have to salvage every year.

Know that I love you and wish you only the best. I am asking for just a little money to get on my feet so I can still have the savings from my mom for emergencies. I pray that you will be kind and do that for me. Pat

She went back to Mikes and would stay in his guest room until her lawyer sent signed copies and next steps to her at his place.

Three days later the doorbell rang at about six that night and Mike knocked on Pat's door, asking her to come to the kitchen. She heard voices and assumed it was someone from the restaurant bringing food. She was so wrong and shocked. It was Robert.

"What are you doing here? How did you find me? What do you want?" Pat asked in rapid succession without stopping for the answers. She stood next to Mike for a little security since she didn't know what Robert would do.

He looked at her and then at Mike and back at her. He could see they were very comfortable together and she could see him bite his lip in anger. Pat took a moment to notice that Robert and Mike were about the same height; Mike was lighter in color and weight. Both were confident men.

Mike was being mean, taunting Robert. "So you are the infamous Robert McKnight. Wow. Not how I pictured you. Why are you at my house?" Robert was angry that he had to come to another man's house for his wife so he told Mike to mind his business.

Mike quickly replied, "I am minding my business. Your business is in my house which now makes your business my business." Robert ignored him and asked Pat to step outside so they could talk in private.

Mike said they didn't have to leave and went to his room. Robert reached for her hands but she pulled back. He was very angry and could barely speak. Finally, he asked quietly "So is he the reason you left me? Why you really want a divorce?"

"No Robert. I explained why in the note I left you. Mike is just a friend who is kind enough to give me a place to stay for a few days."

Robert paused for a moment to decide if he believed her. He chose to focus on what he came to say. "I'm really, really sorry Pat. I told you tax season would be rough and you said you could handle it. You promised. But divorce? We can't talk about it? A divorce is taking this too far."

"I kept my promise to you Robert. You didn't keep your promises to me. I tried to tell you over and over again with notes and messages and flowers and sitting with you and getting into the shower and bringing you a cake."

"You stopped touching me, sitting with me on Sunday or even looking at me. And you didn't call to say hi or check on me during the day anymore, although I understand you talked to Shelly so you weren't too busy. We stopped being connected a long time ago." Pat's voice was sad and sounded just like she felt—hopeless.

"I started wondering if tax season was a cover for cheating on me too since you never came home until really late and you never looked for me. I figured you must be with someone else. I told you from the beginning that I do not compete and you should be with the one you love. That's clearly not me anymore."

His eyes opened wide and his voice got loud "I NEVER, EVER cheated on you. EVER. It was all about work. I am not interested in anyone else. I love YOU. I need YOU. That's why I asked you to be patient. You have to believe me."

He stepped closer to her. "Come home with me Pat, don't do this to us. I need to figure out how to get through tax season with a wife. It's new to me. Give me a chance to figure it out."

She stepped back. "How did you find me?" She asked again, not knowing if he had her followed or had a tracking system on her phone or what.

He responded only by saying, "You are my wife. I will use everything in my power to track you down in whatever city or neighborhood or house you're in." He emphasized the word everything. She knew that was code for 'the FBI has all kinds of resources to find you.'

"I should have noticed what was happening at home

and come for you before now but I was too wrapped up to notice when you left. I deeply regret that. And it took me a few days to find you. Now that I have, let's go home. We need to be together to work through this."

"No thanks Robert," Pat replied, "Remember we've been here before. Me feeling secondary to things and people in your life. I went back to you the first time. Not this time. I said all I had to say in the divorce papers. I just need you to sign and take them to my attorney. I'm tired now so I'm going back to bed. You need to leave. Please. Good night Robert."

He grabbed her arm and pulled her into a bear hug, noticing the weight loss. "Why are you so thin? Are you sick? Did I do this to you?"

Pat looked into his eyes for the first time and he could see the full measure of her pain. She repeated in a whisper "Good night Robert," and walked away.

When he heard Pat's door slam Mike came out of his room, heading for the restaurant. Robert was glad to see that they went in opposite ends of the house to their rooms so he hoped that meant that they were not sleeping together. He was about to walk out the door when Mike took one last jab.

"Really man? She is a wonderful woman. I guess you have your pick of women so maybe you don't think she's all that special. Well she is to regular guys like me. And she doesn't deserve being treated like that. You have killed her spirit. She is not eating. Got her crying in her sleep. I wish she would love me like that. You do not deserve her. Maybe when she gets over you she will give me all that love. I would appreciate it. And I don't have tax seasons."

Robert did not turn around to look at Mike as he spoke, nor did he respond. Finally, he walked out to his truck.

At five a.m. Mike was knocking on Pat's door again. "Come out here Pat." She knew something had to be wrong for him to call her Pat and not Lush, and wake her up when he's just getting in from closing the restaurant.

Her heart started beating fast. "What is it? What's wrong?" She asked repeatedly while she put on a robe.

Robert was standing in the family room. He had never left Mikes house. It had been almost twelve hours.

"What's going on?" Pat was looking from one man to the other. Mike answered for them both: "He's been right outside throughout the night. All he said was he would not leave you. Sit down Pat. This is crazy."

She was staring at Robert because he looked scary, like he was in a trance. Then he focused his eyes on her. She knew he was jealous and hurt and just plain mad at seeing her with Mike. She could also imagine his demeanor when he was on a special assignment, with a deadly focus on his target just before he shot them.

"I've been married before," Mike said, "and it's not easy. It's especially hard when you jump into it on faith and don't really know each other. But here we are. You are like two sick puppies. You need to go home and heal each other and talk and figure it all out."

Pat was about to protest and he stopped her. "You love this man. That is why you are so hurt and can't eat or sleep. And here he is losing sleep and risking arrest because he didn't pay attention to you when he should have. He obviously loves you. Pat, you will always have a place here with me. But the next time you come, you have to really be done with him and be prepared to be with me."

When he heard that Robert turned to look Mike up and down, then back at her. Pat didn't know if he was thinking what she was thinking, but she thought Mike was mighty bold in making that statement right in the face of the man whose wife he said he wanted. And yet Pat felt that Robert needed to know that he couldn't ignore her, for work or any other reason. Somebody wanted her even if he didn't.

"And as for you Mr. McKnight, for the record, you need to know that Pat is my friend. I have never kissed or made love to her. And the only reason I know she cries in her sleep is because she dozed off while we were watching a movie out here one night and started crying.

"I get my share of women so I don't take advantage of hurting souls. And rest assured, she hasn't been with anyone else since you started ignoring her because she's either been at my restaurant or, for the last several days, here in my guest room. Alone."

Mike looked at Pat and said again, "Get your things and go with your husband Pat. Talk it out. Fight it out. Work it out. Give it your best shot. If it doesn't work out, you know where to find me."

Pat went back to the guest room but she wouldn't pack. She started crying and crawled into bed with her back to the door. Mike came in the room and sat on the bed to get her to get up and get packed. She tried to reason with him: "Please don't make me go with him. Just let me stay another couple of days. He will sign the papers by then and I will head back to Houston."

Mike shook his head. Watching her cry made him want to climb in the bed and hold her and assure her that she was loved and he would take care of her. He was angry at Robert for mistreating her and wanted to punch him like high schoolers fighting over the pretty cheerleader. But Pat was the priority, not beating Robert. Mike didn't want her in the heat of a bad moment. He wanted her to make a conscious decision to be with him. He tried to reason with her again. "You know I don't want you to go, that I want you here with me. But you need to get your business straight with him."

Pat lashed out. "He's only here because tax season is over and all of a sudden I'm missing so he has to hunt me down. That is not love. That is convenience and control. He lied to me. He promised to love and take care of me and keep me from feeling alone and unloved. I wouldn't be here if he actually did that. I cannot go through this again with him. This is the second time he's made it clear that I don't matter when he has other priorities."

She paused to catch her breath then started again. "Please Mike, don't make me go. I know I've probably been here too long interrupting your life, and I can leave for Houston tomorrow, but I would rather be with you tonight. You don't let me feel alone and unworthy." She cried so hard her eyes were swollen into little slits and she could barely see.

Mike shared with her his take on men: "Listen to me Pat. If a man will come to another man's house to beg for his woman, he loves her. It is humiliating for a man to know that his woman chose another man over him for any reason, much less for a problem that he caused. Make him earn back your trust. Didn't you say he had a special gift for you once his work was done? At least stay to see what that is. Give it a good try to forgive him.

"If it doesn't work, then don't go to Houston. Come back here and let me love you and take care of you. I know you don't love me like you love him, but I know you love me as a friend so I'll take that until you grow to really love me as your man."

Pat chose not to respond directly to his comments. Her cries softened and she kept repeating, almost in a whisper, "He doesn't love me. I can't do this anymore. Don't make me go Mike. Please."

Robert had eased down the hall toward the voices and stood in the doorway watching and listening to their conversation. Listening to Pat beg Mike to let her stay with him was a knife to his heart and it twisted every time she spoke. Mike stood up to leave the room when he saw Robert. He walked into the hallway and said, "I'm going to sleep. If she is here when I wake up, she is staying with me and I am moving her down the hall into my bed and I'll send movers to get what she wants out of your house by the end of the week. You've got a few hours to decide. Just close the door on your way out."

Robert knew there was nothing to decide. She was leaving with him. He got a towel from the adjoining bathroom, wet it with cold water, then took off his shoes and climbed into bed with her, pulling her to him so that her face was on his chest. She couldn't see through her swollen eyes, but she could smell that it was Robert, which increased her tears and begging. "Please let me go. I can't do this with you anymore. I just want to stay here. Please Robert."

Robert put the cold towel on her eyes and started rocking her in his arms. He was crying too. He never said a word. No apology. No words of comfort. No anger for her being with Mike. They cried together for a half hour, until all of their tears were gone and she fell asleep. He quietly got up and put his shoes back on, put the wet towel in the bathroom, and packed everything of hers that he found in the bedroom and bathroom. He put her bag in their SUV and came back in to get her, picking her up while she was still asleep to take her home.

CHAPTER THIRTY-ONE

When they got back to the house Robert laid Pat on their bed and got the shower ready. He wanted to wash the smell of Mike's house and Mike's bed – even though thankfully it was his guestroom bed — off of her and give them a new start. He woke her up so they could shower together then dried her off and put fresh nightclothes on her.

She was despondent, asking, "Why do you want to hurt me Robert? I told you up front that I needed for us to always be connected to trust that you loved me. You stopped. Then you didn't even respond when I tried to get your attention. Just like before at the restaurant. What did I do to you to make you treat me so bad? Let me go Robert. I'll go quietly. Just let me have the money from my mom and the money Eric gave me. I don't even want your money. I just want to go." Robert felt crushed again and got in the bed to hold and rock her for the rest of the day and into the night.

The next day Robert took a leave of absence from work and spoke with Howard and Frank about the ongoing assignments and who would report to whom. When Pat woke up she went into the kitchen for water and saw the divorce papers had been thrown all over the floor of the kitchen. She went to the guest room that had all the bedroom furniture from her apartment. She was emotionally and physically exhausted and just wanted to get back to sleep in familiar, comfortable surroundings.

When Robert was done with his work call in the office, he went to their bedroom to be with Pat but she was not there or in the family or media rooms. He found her in one of the guest rooms in the dark. He went quietly into the room and sat in the chair by the bed. He finally woke her up with food but she only took a couple of bites and went back to sleep.

She started crying in her sleep and he climbed in bed, wrapping his body around her like he used to. Only this time it felt like he was holding on for dear life, to keep her from leaving him.

For the next two days they slept like that, he cooked and brought food to the room and held her. When she took a shower, he bathed her. He held her and kissed her forehead and eyes and nose and cheeks. She had stopped crying. No tears left. She also stopped looking at him. Between the anger and hurt, not even the Panther Heat and love could make her want to look at the man who caused her such pain.

When Pat asked about work, Robert said he was not leaving her until they got to a better place. However long that took. She was hoping he would leave so she could plan how to get packed up and back to Houston. That was her new goal. She didn't want to fight about it. She wanted to leave and it was just a matter of time.

He asked about her family. They loved to text and for once she was glad because she could hide the pain in her voice. She told them they were hibernating after tax season and she would be in touch.

On May 10th, Shelly and Tommy were ringing the bell early in the morning. She said she had never had a birthday without her brother and knew something drastic was wrong because they both had stopped answering her calls. TJ was staying with friends so they came see for themselves what was going on.

Robert told them the truth. "I messed up, and became absorbed in tax season and didn't take care of my marriage. Pat has asked me for a divorce."

Shelly demanded to see her, calling "Pat, Pat," and looking toward the master bedroom door. Pat never responded so Shelly got up to find her. Robert pointed to the guest room. When Shelly saw Pat in the bed she knew immediately that Pat was depressed and had lost too much weight.

Shelly was sad for what she could see was a lot of pain on Robert's face and Pat's. Tommy asked to pray for them. He prayed for open communication, compassion and understanding, healing, and rededication to one another and to their marriage. When he was finished, Robert asked Shelly to stay with Pat while he and Tommy went to get her car from Mike's house. Shelly stayed in the room with Pat and tried to talk to her but Pat had very little to say.

Robert and Tommy came back with Pat's car and lunch but it was a very somber atmosphere so they ate lunch and Shelly's 7Up pound cake mostly in silence except for updates on TJ. The afternoon was quiet too. Pat asked them to excuse her and went back to bed while the rest of them sat in the kitchen talking. Finally, Robert wished Shelly a Happy Birthday then told them he loved them, but they needed to leave so he could be with his wife. Shelly asked what he was going to do and he replied, "Love her back to me. I don't have anything else." They left.

The next morning at about three a.m. they were both awake. He asked about Mike, and what did he mean to her that she went immediately to his house to get away from home. "You didn't go to your family or even a hotel. Why him Pat? Why another man?" He sounded dejected.

She answered him in a monotone voice, not interested in whether he believed her or not, just giving him the facts, her rationale for not going to Yvonne and Howards, with family or a hotel, or even with her friends at FEAST, Brookes or Willis. She wanted him to know it was not an easy decision. She repeated what Mike had said, that they were just friends, and added that he was very nice to her when she felt abandoned and alone. She also told him that she needed to be with somebody to stop feeling so alone and hurt and being with a friend helped. The friend just happened to be Mike.

Robert said he was truly sorry he had made her feel that way and assured her that he thought of her every day. He said again that he was just very busy and had a lot of pressure on him for the company. "By the time I got home, I was too tired and stressed to even give you the moment you asked for. That was wrong. You only asked for a minute. And by Sunday I was completely on empty so the best I could do was sleep and hope to refill my empty tank and get ready for the next week.

"But for the record," he announced, "Mike made it very clear that he loves you like I love you. He wants to do things for you that a man wants to do for his woman or wife so don't think that I'm buying that friend story."

Pat was angry. "I know how he feels Robert. But I don't love him like that. And he knows that. I compartmentalized him and my relationship with him so that it didn't cross the line or interfere with our marriage. I needed you to understand and trust me. But what does it matter what Mike feels or what I feel for Mike? You left me alone and lonely again. Only this time instead of for a woman and child it was for tax season. It's just one hit after another with you. What's next Robert? Never mind. I don't want to know and I don't want to find out." She knew what she was saying was mean, but she wanted Robert to hurt like she was hurting.

He spent the next few days trying to draw her out in conversation but she had very little to say. She would barely look at him. When she did look at him, he saw that the light in her eyes that she used to have for him was gone. She was going through the motions and he had a feeling that one day he would come home and she would be gone. The thought crushed him but made him resolve to fight harder for her. For them.

He admitted to her that, "In twenty or so years, for as many women as I have dated or hooked up with, I am still a novice in the relationship department. I have never loved anyone the way I love you and I've never had to work at having a serious, long-term relationship. You are my first and I'm hoping my only. I have screwed up and I understand why you are angry and want to leave me. But know this: I do love you. Very much. In my own clumsy, inadequate, unskilled way. There has not been a moment since I've met you that I didn't think that we should be together forever. That's why I asked you to marry me right away. I'm hoping that you will work with me to get it right. And very soon." He tried to get a smile out of her with the 'very soon' but it did not happen.

On Thursday, Robert called for Pat to come to the kitchen for lunch. Next to her plate was a gift-wrapped box. Inside was her post tax season gift—tickets to a seven day jazz cruise with all her favorite musicians and singers on board. It was two weeks away but he had bought the tickets in February, just when things were starting to change. Ordinarily she would be thrilled since she loved cruises and of course smooth jazz. This time, however, she was not convinced they would still be together and it showed on her face. He was more optimistic.

He wanted them to start dating again, saying they both could use some fresh air. They went to the flower show and were surrounded by the beauty of all the different colors of flowers and vases and the beautiful arrangements. It was nice and lifted their spirits, but Pat was still quiet with him.

Over the next ten days, excursions took them to the aquarium and then the zoo and the Black History Museum and a few restaurants. They were tourists in their hometown.

While Pat felt better physically and the outings were nice, every time she looked at him she remembered the weight in her chest from being disappointed and feeling rejected. And she knew that in a few months it would be tax season again and she wanted no part of that.

He asked her to focus on one day at a time and prepare for the cruise. Turns out Howard and Yvonne were going too. Frank didn't want to spend a whole week with any one female so he volunteered to stay back and cover the office.

The suite was beautiful, a big room decorated in soft pastel colors. The tables were glass and brass. There was a king sized four poster brass bed and a large white marble and glass and brass bathroom with a bathtub that could definitely fit the two of them. The veranda was huge, bigger than the room, and since it was on the end of the ship, it wrapped around to the other side of the ship. They could easily have a party for fifty people on it. She hoped that with a few days on the veranda, looking at the calm blue water, maybe her heart would slowly start healing. She hoped her countenance in public showed quiet and thoughtful, not destroyed by the love of her life. She had turned her phone off after moving to Mike's so she had not spoken to anyone for more than two weeks.

Yvonne was very happy to see her with Robert and

told Pat that she missed her, and Howard had said that Robert was devastated and had taken a leave of absence to be with her and fix things. The music was soothing and helped her not be so anxious.

On the last night, Brian Culbertson was the featured artist. The group had a great table with Robert and Pat sitting on the front, closest to the musicians. When Brian got to Pat's favorite songs, he asked Patricia McKnight to identify herself. She looked at Robert and he just smiled.

She raised her hand and Brian dedicated the songs to her from her husband "who loves you in every season, and asks that you never, ever forget." Pat was stunned and kept looking at Robert while he rubbed her arm and held her hand.

When the set was over Brian came to their table and gave Pat the letter that Robert had written explaining how they were newlyweds who had met and married the same day, and this cruise was 'our honeymoon and gift for surviving tax season.' In the letter, Robert told how he was introduced to Brian's music because his wife played it almost every day, especially her three favorites, so would he please, please dedicate them to her.

Brian had written a note on the letter saying he was delighted to do this because he believed in love and that is what all of his songs are about. He also gave Pat a couple of his tour t-shirts.

The men around them groaned at Robert saying he had raised the bar so high none of them could compete in doing something nice for their wives. Truth be told,

Pat's heart melted a little bit when she saw the letter was dated in March, when things had fully unraveled for her. Her heart skipped a beat when she thought 'He really had been thinking of me!'

Robert was looking for signs that she might be forgiving him and she was starting to realize the cruise was over and they were about to return to their normal lives. Some decisions still needed to be made.

She thought that in all fairness, he deserved something for giving her such a nice evening and great trip but she was not sure she was ready to be all in again.

While they were leaving the theatre, Robert asked her if there was anything else she wanted to see or do on the ship since it was their last night.

Pat whispered in his ear "Yes, actually. It would be a shame to have had that fabulous suite and we never christened it. So I want us to go back there and have sex. Would you be interested in doing that?" Making love was never an issue for them. Even in her anger and hurt, she missed his body and the way he made her body feel.

A big grin spread over his face and he said "Yes! Very much! I have missed you too."

Then he frowned and whispered "but I didn't bring condoms. We ran out in January then I got busy with work. Before the cruise I was focused on keeping us together and you know it's been a while since we made love. Let me stop at the store and see if they have any."

"So are you telling me that you really did cheat on me and we have to use condoms?"

"NO. NO. Not at all. NEVER." He was getting loud

and people turned to look.

"Well then, Mr. McKnight." Pat whispered. "I am your wife and I am on birth control. And I'm asking you to have sex with me. So if you want what I'm offering, you need to follow me right now. No detours."

When they got back to their suite she stripped quickly, leaving only her heels on, and took a sheet and blanket out to the veranda. It was pitch black outside and no one could see or hear them from the upper or lower floors or next door. It was a very quiet night.

The chaise was oversized with a thick cushion. Pat covered it with the blanket then the sheet, and laid back with a leg draped over each arm of the chaise and her hands over her head, holding the top of the cushion.

It only took a few moments for Robert to come out searching for her in the dark. When his eyes adjusted, he saw her open and ready for him. There was a nice, warm tropical breeze blowing and they both could feel the wind on their naked bodies. It was sexy and intoxicating.

He climbed onto the chaise and kissed her with such intensity and depth it felt like he thought this would be their last kiss. She knew her lips and tongue would be swollen, but didn't care. She had missed kissing him too. Then he positioned himself inside her ever so slowly. Skin to skin contact was totally different from wearing a condom. It felt really good and they paused at every inch he put in her to enjoy the feeling. In no time he had that look on his face again. Passionate beast. Lust and love.

Pat wrapped her legs around his head to get the best possible penetration as he braced himself on his knees.

Slow and steady they moved together. Without breaking apart she put her legs down and turned over and he laid on her back, licking and biting her shoulders and neck, squeezing her breasts and grabbing her hair, never missing a beat inside her.

He whispered in her ear, "You're damn good at what you do to me Pat. I have missed you."

She squeezed her muscles like women do in Kegel exercises to milk him slowly and his mumbling started. "I. You. Love. Oh. Please. Ahh. God. Yes. Yes." Before Pat knew it she was moaning for Bobby and he responded with a hiss and a deep moan of his own. Afterwards he commented, "Well, that was some kind of wonderful. Your mind and body never cease to amaze and excite me. Thank you."

They agreed to go inside and pack and get dressed then go back outside to watch the sun come up. She asked to talk first so they sat facing each other. Her expression was solemn.

"Thank you for coming to get me Robert. And for being so sweet and so determined to make me feel better these last few weeks. And the cruise? It has been a nice week. I would like it though if we could agree not to talk about what happened anymore. No more apologies or doing things to make up to me. I need to stop thinking about it and hurting. I just want things to keep moving between us naturally. I'm trying hard to trust you not to do this to me again, not to forget about me. But it's hard. I don't know that I can. Do you understand what I'm saying?"

He was very quiet and held her hands, looking into her eyes. "Yes, I understand. I will not do that again. Really. I promise."

They went inside to pack then took a bath together in the big tub. When they got out, Robert wrapped a towel around her and picked her up, placing her in the center of the bed.

He started rubbing her body and making love to her all over again. Only this time it felt different from earlier in the night. She could feel the pressure in his hands and his tongue as he kissed her and sucked her nipples and moved between her legs. He felt almost like a savage about to ravish his victim, a firm grip on her arms and legs.

By the time he entered her he was whispering, "I love you Pat. I need you. All of you. Everyday. All of you. We belong together. You are mine."

He pounded inside her with a vengeance. Rough. When they were finished Pat could barely move and they only had a few minutes to see the sunrise and leave. She was thinking 'At least I didn't cry this time. I have shed enough tears. But I definitely enjoyed every unexpected moment of that session.'

Before they left the room for the last time Robert asked: "Can I say something? I know you asked me if I wanted to have sex with you and I was so happy to hear that you wanted us together that way that I didn't say this then. What we do together is not sex to me. I only make love to you. To use the word sex for us is insufficient for what we share. Even when I get a little carried away like tonight. It's because I love you and missed you but it was still making love. Okay?" Pat nodded yes.

At the airport, while waiting for their flight home, Robert kept saying, "This was a great week. A really great week. Maybe we need to do this cruise every year after tax season. That room and that veranda are good for rejuvenating the soul." Pat never responded.

When they got back home Robert saw that she was distant and quiet. The undercurrent of sadness was still there. To family and other people she was pleasant and polite. But in their house she still had nothing to say to him. He asked her to come back to their bed, saying he missed her and it felt good to sleep with her again on the cruise. He also asked if they could cook and eat together. She obliged him. Then she would go to the office or media room to be away from him and alone. He asked her why she did that when before they always went to the family room to hang out together. She said she thought since they were home together all day now that he might want some quiet time, some alone time. He assured her "I was alone for forty years. I want to be with you every chance I get." When she went to the office she was usually writing so he left her alone. Whenever she went to the media room he would go in there with her. They read or watched movies, even a couple of romance ones, while he sat close to her.

Robert finally went back to work after a month off. She was not whole but much better. At the end of that first week Robert pulled out the divorce papers and tore them up, saying "I know you said don't talk about what happened again, but here's the thing: divorce is not and cannot be an option for us. I adore you. I absolutely love you and all that you bring to my life. I need to take care of you. Plus I know you love me. You cannot leave me. We are in this together forever.

"I know this year was tough," he acknowledged. "But I'm an accountant and tax season is part of our lives so we have to figure out how to live through it until I retire. And just so you know, I have already made changes to my team, giving each person more responsibility so that I just review and approve all documents. I can see that they are up to the responsibility and I need to stop using work as a shield for my personal issues. So we are done with this, right?"

Pat never responded, still in the 'wait and see' mode.

CHAPTER THIRTY-TWO

One Friday afternoon Pat got a call from Robert. Elliott and Dexter were in town and he wanted the guys to stay with them, and he wanted to invite Howard and Frank over that night. It had been a long time since they had all been together.

Of course she said yes, then went into panic mode, making sure the house was ready and ordering food. There was no way she was going to try to cook for that group on the first meeting. She set dishes out and made a salad then went to the store to get more beer, some snacks and breakfast food, and pick up the dinner and dessert she had ordered.

Robert heard the garage door open and saw her come to the family room. He smiled at her from across the room, clearly happy that his brothers were all together again and that she would finally meet the last two.

She saw them all sprawled out in the family room, on the sofa, on the floor, in the chair. They were in jeans and t-shirts or hoodies. A very nice looking group and each one was definitely in great physical shape. They were talking about their recent travels and giving family updates and didn't hear her come in. They were in a 'safe zone' and had let down their guard.

Pat stood in the doorway looking around until they noticed her. They got quiet so she said "My, my, my, this is a lot of manhood in one room. Our home will never be the same."

They all laughed and Howard and Frank were the first to speak to here. "Hey Sis" they said in unison.

Robert knew that there was stuff to bring in from the car so he asked for help and they all jumped up immediately. As they walked by, he introduced them. "Elliott, Dex, this is my wife, Patricia."

Elliott was over six feet tall and slender with a full beard and mustache covering his mocha face. Dexter was close to six feet four, very dark skinned and thick, but toned, tight. With a mustache but no other facial hair.

Each one gave Pat a hug and said that like Howard and Frank, they were blown away that Robert was married, but happy for them. They all said they were enjoying the home that Robert and Pat had made together. Warm and cozy, they could feel the love.

They each told Pat to get their number from Robert and make sure to call them if she or he ever needed anything. Anytime, day or night.

She was invited to sit with them while they ate which was great because she could get to know them and watch how they interacted. They asked how Robert and Pat met so Pat asked Robert to tell the story. She wanted to hear how he would describe their meeting and getting to today.

He was happy to tell them, "I was standing outside

the restaurant talking to Howard and Frank on my birthday when this silver Lexus pulled up catching my attention. Then all I saw in front of me were these pretty legs in a short skirt and high heel shoes. By the time I got to her face I was already planning that I was going to get to know her. She's a writer and got some good news, a book deal, and started jumping up and down and squealing with happiness and I had all kind of visions of making her squeal like that for me."

Pat was shocked and embarrassed, turning beet red, covering her face then punching him on his leg.

They all laughed and he continued. "I got her to have dinner with me and my family so I could see if she had some brains behind that beauty. She charmed us ALL, me, Shelly, Tommy, and even TJ stopped playing his video games to talk to her! I heard the cuffs click and knew I was done. And that was fine with me. I was real happy about it."

The guys all laughed but Pat didn't know what he meant by the 'cuffs click' so she asked him. He said "Handcuffs baby. I was on lock with you forever and I knew it immediately." Pat blushed again. He leaned over to give her a quick kiss on her forehead.

He continued the story. "She tried to act all cool like she didn't want to intrude and needed to leave but I charmed her in to going to Shelly's for dessert. I knew I had her then. And you know how women are, they want you to chase them and date them but I cut through all of that by asking her to marry me that night. She freaked out a little, but I held her tight and put The Hawk eyes on her until she finally said yes. Tommy married us and we have been together ever since."

They all looked at Pat, smiling and teasing him saying, "The Hawk swooped in to get his own wings clipped. Wow man. This is a first. Congratulations."

Then they told her about the names they adopted when they created their brotherhood. All animal names that related to their skills. That is how they sometimes talked in the field and definitely in private to each other.

Robert was "Hawk" or "The Hawk" because he studied people and their personalities and actions and knew exactly how to get what he wanted from the 'target.' He could quickly spot a liar or enemy. In addition, he was a sharpshooter, so when it was time to take someone down, he got the job. Robert didn't crack a smile as he looked at Pat and said "those skills came in mighty handy the night we met."

Howard was "Goat" because he was very smart and could find the weirdest piece of information, the needle in the haystack that brought a case together.

They called Frank "Wolf" because he was very intelligent, fearless, and always the first to attack.

Elliott was "Shark" because he was unparalleled when it came to asking the right insightful questions and eliciting information from people. And he didn't take no for an answer.

Dexter was "Bear" because of his size and because people saw the former pro football player as soft and cuddly which gave him an advantage when people underestimated his intelligence and talked too much in front of him. And he could move quickly and tackle anyone of any size before they could get away.

Pat asked how they met. Frank shared the story of how they all showed up at Quantico on the first day and found themselves assigned to the same dorm floor. Coincidentally, their rooms were all at the same end of the hall. "We just clicked, in and out of each other's rooms and sharing life stories. Like a lot of men we bonded over watching sports, and we also played ball together to stay in shape. We helped each other in our classes and did a lot of role playing with each other to help learn some of the tricks of assessing a situation, interrogation, and how to respond in a crisis. We learned each others strengths and weaknesses so we knew how to help each other in the field. Over time, we were paired with each other in training exercises as well as for our first few special assignments. There was never a question that we had each others' backs for the rest of our lives."

All of the guys nodded yes to what Frank was saying and you could tell from their pensive faces that they were thinking of some tough experiences in the field. To get them back to a happy place Pat asked if she could take some pictures of this historic night. They all went into a variety of poses while she got candid shots, then there was the serious one of the five of them standing together. Brothers for life.

Then they asked Pat, "When can we read your books?" She brought out a copy of each of the novellas, saying, "Remember, it's all fiction, made up stories." She could not imagine what they would think of her after reading all the sex parts if, like Robert, they thought she might have done some of those things.

Finally she left them to clean the kitchen and set up dessert and snacks when Robert came out to her to ask if she was ok with Elliott and Dexter staying for a few days. They would cook their own food or eat out and clean up behind themselves and not interrupt her days.

Pat knew it was love and respect between them and now her so she was fine with all of that. As she headed for bed to give them their evening to talk, Pat kept thinking that her single girlfriends in Houston and Chicago would really like Frank or Dexter or Elliot, all fine hunks of chocolate. Maybe someday she and Robert would be able to get them all together.

The next morning Pat got up while the guys slept and started breakfast, cooking bacon and sausage and grits and making pancake batter so some things would be done already and they could get whatever else they wanted to make a meal.

As she was eating her breakfast, Elliott came out and sat with her. He wanted to be sure she really loved Robert and was not trying to take advantage of him because he had money and was lonely. The Shark was on the case, asking questions trying to get to know her.

Pat answered honestly by giving him her brief resume as a mid-western girl with mid-western values of education, hard work and helping others, and strong family roots.

"My desire to love and be loved is because that's what Harris' do. And that's what I needed after the number of family losses in my life. With Robert's southern values and family background being so similar, it was not hard to grow to love him. Besides, you know how he is. Once he decides what he wants, there is no way to say no. It took me a minute to not be afraid of his boldness, but I finally said yes. Robert will tell you that it's not about his money for me. That has never been a driver except for me to have enough to live a decent life. I was doing that on my own."

She then countered with her own questions to understand more about who he was.

He was from an elite family in Washington, DC whose dedication to the United States and helping others in America started with his great, great grandfather. All of the men on his father's side, and even a couple of the women, had been in some branch of the Department of Defense, including the military and the ATF (Alcohol, Tobacco and Firearms). He was the only one that chose the FBI. He was definitely planning to be a 'lifer' with the bureau, but said he would appreciate having his own great love someday to round out his life. Maybe after he was done with the various assignments.

Finally satisfied that she really loved Robert and was good for him, he fixed his breakfast and went to the family room just as Dexter came out.

Dexter turned out to really be a big teddy bear, a very caring man with a loving heart, but Pat could hear the undertone of seriousness, bordering on meanness, on a couple of calls she overheard with his family who constantly called about money.

They talked for a long time about his life growing up in Alabama, with a single Mom and a couple of sisters who depended on him often through the years for money and time to take them places and help with men problems. He cultivated a good listening ear, a soft spot for women in need, and an intolerance for the men who mistreated them.

He liked being in the bureau because "it created the family of brothers that I never had and never knew I needed until I met these guys and we went through some assignments together."

He admired and respected Robert's intelligence, maturity, and heart so his attitude was that if Hawk loved her, he loved her too, and any other details could be provided on a need to know basis.

Frank had spent the night too, wanting to spend as much time as possible with his brothers. He was very serious for a change and confessed to Pat that he was an orphan who had been in a few foster homes but never adopted. When he aged out of the system at eighteen he found his way to college and a dorm room, using his acumen with numbers to get a degree in accounting. Then he went into the Air Force, then the FBI. These places provided him work, a place to live that he could call home, and some semblance of family that helped with his sense of aloneness. He also had serious anger issues that were generally kept in check because of the regimen and rules he had to follow.

It was his life with no loved ones, as kind of a nomad, and his anger that made him what he called "the perfect candidate for special assignments." He approached them all with a ruthlessness that was frightening to some but often helped when all other options had been exhausted. That's why he never settled down with a woman. He never had that kind of love and was actually afraid to try. He did not want another rejection in his life. And he didn't want to get killed and leave someone hurting. He had been hurt enough and didn't want to do that to anyone else. But he loved Robert, Howard, Elliott, and Dexter, and knew that they loved him. He would do whatever he needed to do for them any time they needed him, or if anyone hurt them.

Howard, the elder statesman from New York, the only married man, had gone home. Yvonne was the love of his life and he always went home to her. He was the one with the idea to start their own firm. After he and Yvonne got married, he did not want to leave her for such dangerous work. He had done only one so far since the company opened and he was trying to make that his last one. They were starting to talk about having a family so he wanted to be there to see his kid or kids grow up.

By the time breakfast was over Pat was 'Sis,' Little Sis,' or 'Sista Pat' to all of them.

Yvonne and Pat decided to give the guys a night for themselves and spend some time together with their own girls night for massages and mani/pedi's so Yvonne booked a night at one of the downtown hotels. When Pat went to the bedroom and announced to Robert that she was leaving for a spa night with Yvonne so he and his friends could have a guy's night out as well as have privacy to talk at home without her in the shadows, she did not get the reaction of appreciation that she expected.

He frowned and said, "We do not need any privacy and if you don't like my friends, just say that. They can stay somewhere else. I want you home with me." Then he asked, "Are you really going with Yvonne or am I going to have to go back to Mike's or some other man's house to get you and bring you home?" He heard Pat gasp. She felt like she had been slapped, but that didn't stop him. He finished by saying, "And just so you understand, I know Yvonne is no saint given what she did the first year of their marriage so don't use her as a cover for your secret activities."

She looked in his face and finally realized that the wounds from the end of tax season had not healed completely for him either. For the first time she saw insecurity in him so she asked if trust was now a problem in our marriage. "Do you trust me Robert? Do you really believe that I will cheat on you? Are you saying that I can't ever have a girls night out? Or go to Chicago or Houston or anywhere out of town for a week-end with my girlfriends?"

His only response was "I just want you home with me, not in some hotel with someone else. But you are a grown, independent woman. Do whatever you want to do." With that, he pulled the door open and started to walk out of the room, but Pat stepped in between him and the door and kicked the door shut. She was angry and ready to let him know.

"No, no, no, no, no. You do not get to say vile things

to me then walk out the door as if you are the cock of the walk. Who do you think you are? Let me remind you of something before you go Robert." Her voice was very low, but also very stern. "The reason you had to come to Mike's to get me was because you were not on your job being the husband you should have been to me. Remember? For weeks you ignored me, acting like I didn't exist. Not talking to me, not trying to stay connected to me. Left me to my own devices. You clearly did not care. But I was faithful to you. I didn't sleep with Mike or anyone else. And yes, I could have. You're not the only one in this house who is attractive to other people. And just so you know, Yvonne was nowhere around. I don't need Yvonne or anyone else to cover for me. I am very capable of doing what I need to do by myself. Don't forget, I was by myself the night I met you.

"Let me also remind you that I am your wife, not some random chick you had a drive-by with, so do not ever talk to me like that again. EVER. If you don't trust me then we don't have a marriage and I will have my lawyer reprint those divorce papers. You need to decide by the time Elliott and Dexter leave here because I will not hang around to be abused by you, verbally, emotionally, or physically."

He was shocked to hear her talk to him like that and stood frozen trying to process what was happening. She didn't think anyone, especially a woman, had ever spoken to him like that before. She did not let him respond, grabbing her purse and cell phone and walking out the bedroom door, slamming it behind her.

She went to the kitchen for a bottle of water and slammed the refrigerator door. Elliott and Dexter were still sitting at the island and turned to look at her then at the master bedroom door and back at her.

"Have a good day gentlemen," she said, slamming the garage door on the way out.

By nature Pat was the quiet one, always trying to work with people to talk through issues and make peace. She usually didn't get so angry until she felt that people took her kindness for weakness or talked to her like she was stupid. She was already on edge, so Robert's comments hit a nerve and he needed to understand that she had another side to that kind nature and today was the day for him to find out about it.

Pat called Yvonne from the car and told her that she had to change their plans. Yvonne was disappointed but did not question her, probably hearing something in her voice that said she was in a bad mood. They talked for a few minutes about Yvonne's week and the people on her job and her family. She was good at telling stories and always knew how to make Pat feel better without knowing why she was feeling bad. That's a friend. They had a good laugh about the reaction of the women when those five hunks of chocolate descended upon the restaurant or bar together.

She decided to go to the zoo for a couple of hours to walk off some of her anger and calm down to think clearly. Looking at the animals reminded her of how simple life can and should be and how she wanted that kind of life. Finally, she got some food and headed home.

When the guys came home to shower and change

clothes for their night out Pat was in bed asleep. Robert came into the room and was surprised and very happy to see her there. He got in bed by climbing on top of her in his sweaty gym clothes and woke her up to apologize for being such a jerk, saying horrible things, and making her think he didn't trust her.

"I was being selfish and mean and yes, still a little jealous about you being at Mikes and wanting to stay with him instead of coming home. I'm sorry. It just felt good having you and all the guys here at the same time. It felt like I had a family again and my family was all together and I didn't want anything to change the dynamic and how I was feeling. It has been a long time since I felt like this. I should have said that instead of what I did say. I do trust you. With my life. And of course you can have girls nights and weekends. I'm sorry I said those things and promise not to say them again. If it's not too late, call Yvonne and go to the hotel. Have a good time. I'll pay for everything for both of you. Just don't be mad at me. Besides, you know how grumpy I get when I don't get my Morning Magic. This has been a crazy day and is about to be a wild night. I need to know that we are good before I leave. Are we good?"

She never responded to his apology, telling him to "Just go." He turned her face to his so he could look into her eyes and assure her that although he could be foolish sometimes, like he was earlier, he was really sorry and definitely would not talk to her like that again. Then, to try to lighten the mood, he asked, "Would you tell that exorcist lady that spoke to me earlier out of your mouth to please go back into hibernation or wherever she came from. She was mean and I do not want to hear from her again." Pat had to smile at that.

She decided not to call Yvonne about going to the hotel and stayed in bed. When Robert came home late that night, he was alone. He said the guys thought he needed privacy to grovel to her so Howard went home and the other three each found some woman to be with for the night. They had the house to themselves. They had make up sex and enjoyed sleeping late for a change.

For the next few days, she hung out with Elliott and Dexter while Robert, Howard, and Frank were at the office. In the mornings, she worked in the office while they slept or read or watched television. They went to the gym with her in the afternoon so that they could work out too, and they talked and played cards and board games and started dinner until Robert came home. Howard and Frank came by after work every day too. They all seemed content being together for whatever time they had. They were happy that Robert and Pat were talking again too.

Elliott and Dexter stayed almost a week then both got a call for another assignment. Pat was sorry to see them go since they were so nice and a distraction from the problems between her and Robert, but she was also glad to let Robert and each of them know they would always have a home with them.

Pat could feel a short story or maybe even a book in the making about these guys and their lives and their friendship. There could never be enough good brotherhood stories.

CHAPTER THIRTY-THREE

After the brothers left, Pat and Robert went back to their regular weekly schedule. Pat was on a September first deadline now and had several edits to make so except for the visits to Houston, they stayed at home.

It was good that Pat was busy because as the months went by she became more nervous about tax season. Robert could feel the tension build in her body and their Morning Magic didn't seem to be enough to relax her. He gave her back rubs and foot rubs and hand massages all while telling her how he had changed things at the office and assured her that things would be different this time. She really wanted to believe him, but those feelings she had the first year still felt very fresh. Her eyes were still void of the light and love she originally had for him and she was still very quiet at home.

For her birthday this year, Robert took her to Carmel-by-the-Sea, California and they rented a car service to drive them up and down the coast. They had in room, side-by-side massages, sat by the fire on the beach outside the hotel, ate at nice restaurants serving delicious food and shopped at quaint shops. It was a romantic time that neither wanted to be over. Pat liked having Robert all to herself because she knew she would soon become secondary again.

They decided to host Thanksgiving as a way to shift the focus from what was coming. Both sides of the families were invited so their house was full. Shelly and Tommy and TJ came up from Houston along with Robert's uncles and their families and cousins Kevin and Alexander, as well as Uncle Roy and Aunt Ginny, and their children Gina and Roy Jr. and his wife and son. Both of Pat's aunts that lived in the Dallas-Ft. Worth area came over with their families. Robert's aunts were on vacation together.

When Frank saw all of Pat's single female cousins he told her she was wrong for not giving him a heads up. They were pretty, smart, and fun women and he was really sorry he had brought a date. But now he knew and would not make that mistake again. He said he might start thinking of actually dating one woman exclusively if it could be one of them.

His eyes kept following Vicky every time she moved. Pat had to tell him a couple of times that he was being obvious and asked him if he needed a bib for the drool. He looked sheepish and said being in this house with all the love between her and Robert, her family and Robert's family, plus Howard and Yvonne made him start feeling some kind of way.

His date noticed that his attention was elsewhere too. She was just trying to hold on to get through the day without him taking her home early or sending her home in an Uber. Then everyone noticed that she had her eye on Kevin so it looked like she was not left out of the romance possibilities.

Vicky knew he was looking at her all day and had a good laugh about it. But she was looking at him too so who knows? It could be a love match someday.

Robert kept laughing and shaking his head, telling Frank, "You don't know what you are in for if you want one of Pat's relatives. They know how to get a fellow without trying and once hooked, there is no turning back."

Pat finally told Frank, "You don't want my cousin. We love hard. You can't mess with her and break her heart like you do with the rest of your casual dates."

He did his best not to stare at Vicky after that but you could tell he was checking her out throughout the evening. He made sure to interact with her, sitting next to her while they ate and asking questions to get to know her. They even danced together a couple of times. He clearly had something serious on his mind for the rest of the night.

Everyone ate and drank and played cards and games and danced until the wee hours. Every room in the house was taken and all the ladies pitched in to keep the food trays full and drinks ready and the kitchen clean.

When the Dallas-Ft. Worth area family and friends were leaving, Frank and Vicky had a moment together to say goodbye. Vicky told him, "I'm flattered at your interest but definitely not your type. I'm not a one-night stand or a drive-by or booty call. I want a relationship, a commitment, not a player." Frank told her he understood and would keep that in mind.

By Saturday afternoon, everyone had gone home and Pat and Robert spent most of the day putting the house back together. She was glad for something to do to keep her mind off the months ahead. Her anxiety about tax season came back with a vengeance. She decided to seek comfort in the place that gave her comfort during the first tax season.

CHAPTER THIRTY-FOUR

Pat stopped by FEAST to visit Mike, Brookes, and Willis, realizing that she missed the sense of family they gave her. She told them that she missed them and appreciated their support. They were happy to see her and quickly got her caught up on what she had missed.

Mike just stared at her, looking for answers to questions that he never asked. She told him she appreciated him and would be forever grateful that he took her in, then pushed her to find out if she had a marriage. And yes, she and Robert were still trying to figure things out, but she needed to be able to come to the bar sometimes too.

He looked sad but said ok, he would take what he could get until she came to her senses and came back to him. He smiled, they hugged, and that made them both feel better.

He also said that Robert had thanked him for being a friend to her and taking care of her when he picked up her car. They knew they could never be friends, but they could be cordial, not enemies.

In her mind Robert respected other men and didn't mind giving a compliment when due. If not for Pat, he and Mike would probably be friends because Mike had integrity and respect for men and their relationships. At the same time Robert's ego probably would not rest until he let Mike know that he had gotten her back and Mike would not get another shot at being with her.

Brookes and Willis told her how they felt so bad seeing her hurting. They saw Robert when he came to talk to Mike about getting her car and said that they believed that if Robert did everything that Mike said, he must love her.

Willis gave Pat a hug and whispered "You're a blessed child. Two handsome men love you." Pat smiled back at her and said with a shrug, "I know. Except I can only be with one. That makes it hard when you know you made somebody unhappy in the end."

Brookes said sadly, "You only get one great love in your life if you are lucky. Make every moment count because one of you could be gone and it would be too late to say you're sorry, make up, or work through the problems."

Pat felt so good with them she started going back regularly to FEAST on Thursday's while Robert was at work and then the gym. But she made sure to be home before he got there.

Brookes and Willis and Pat immediately got back into their rhythm but somehow they had lost Mike. When she asked them what was going on, they said, "he stays in his office a lot, like he used to before you started coming in."

She didn't think much of it because she knew he was

working and he still paid for her food and drinks. But after about a couple of weeks and she hadn't seen him at all, she went in search of answers.

When she knocked on his office door he didn't answer at first, but she heard movement so she knew he was inside. And she knew he could see her on the security cameras. She knocked again and he finally said, "Come in."

"Hey you. Are you okay? Been missing you in the group." She was looking at him but he never looked at her. "I'm fine. Just busy," was his curt reply. "Okay. Well, just wanted you to know we miss you," as she walked toward the door. He never responded, just grunted, "Mmm-hmm."

Another week passed and still no sign of Mike so she goes to his office again. This time the door was ajar and she could see him inside staring at the wall in deep thought. When she knocked, he slowly turned around, looked her up and down and asked, "What do you need? I'm busy."

"Are you mad at me? Did I say or do something wrong? Are you avoiding me?"

"Are you still with your husband?" he asked.

"Yes, but what does that have to do with you hanging out with us? I thought we were friends?"

His only response was, "I'm busy."

When she tried to talk to Brookes and Willis about Mike, they didn't have a comment. Don't bite the hand that feeds you?

For each of the next two weeks when she walked in he was at the bar. When he saw her he would nod then leave the area and go back to his office. Pat knew then there was a real problem so after a couple of drinks she got the courage to march into his office and sit in the chair across from his desk until he looked at her. He said his usual, "I'm busy."

This time she refused to leave until he looked at her and told her what was wrong. "What's happening to you? I hear you have stopped coming out to chat and you're grumpy when you are around. And you are hiding from me. What's really going on? Talk to me please. Is your family ok? Are you sick? I'm worried about you."

He jumped up from his chair, grabbed his jacket and said to Pat, "Let's go."

"Where to?" she asked a little nervously.

"To my house. I need to get something. We can talk there."

They went out the back and got on his motorcycle. He gave her his helmet and made sure she was secure before taking off.

When they got to his house, she got a bottle of water from the kitchen and waited for him in the family room. She was not good on motorcycles and was nervous about the conversation that they were about to have so she needed a minute to calm down and get ready.

Pat began looking at television and got comfortable on the sofa but quickly dozed off. Not sure how long she had been asleep but she started having a very sexy dream. Soft music was playing and it smelled really nice in the room. Someone was kissing her face and neck and opening her top to rub her nipples and caress her breasts. The stroking caused her to moan and she woke up, startled to find Mike kneeling in front of her, thumbs on her nipples and he was kissing and licking the space between her breasts. His mouth was poised to suck her left nipple.

Pat screamed, mostly in anger but also fear, and tried to cover herself but he had her arms pinned to her side. "Mike. Stop. What are you doing? I am married. You can't do this." He had never done anything like this before and she did not understand why he had crossed the line.

"Mike please stop," She begged.

"Don't be frightened," he said softly. "You know I won't hurt you."

"Then why are you doing this to me?" she asked. He kissed and licked between her breasts one last time then closed her top and leaned back, freeing her arms. She crossed them in front of her chest, as if that would guard her from him.

"Listen to me. I love you Pat. I'm in love with you. Damn near obsessed actually. Have been since you first walked into the bar. I love your smile, your laughter, your sense of humor. You're very sexy and smart. And you always smell delicious, even when you are just coming from the gym. I would love to lick the sweat off your body every day.

"I haven't been with another woman since you first came to the bar. I meant what I said about you leaving your husband and coming to be with me so I could take care of you. I have money, a business, and time. I just need you. I think about you every day, all day. About us being together and building a life, travelling, and just hanging out after I get home from work. And making love. Making lots of love.

"There was a moment when I first saw you in the bar that we connected and I knew that even though you are married, there is another side of you, a soft underbelly, an itch in you that only a few men can scratch. It doesn't mean you are a bad person or unfaithful, it just means that you have a layer of sensuality and sexy that is yet to be explored. I don't think your husband has found that part of you yet. So tonight, I wanted to see if I could scratch that itch just a little bit. I just wanted my own moment with you before we said goodbye. I want out of the friend zone with you. I know you love your husband and I respect that and will not interfere. But you have to stay out of FEAST and out of my life so I can move on. The next time you come in, you should be divorced or widowed and prepared to move in with me. Do you understand?"

Pat was in shock at what was happening and trying to process what he was saying.

"Do you understand?" he asked again, louder.

"Yes," she finally whispered.

He got up off the floor and pulled her up, grabbed his jacket and helmet, and they walked out the door. When he dropped her off at her car, he made his final statement. "I'm sorry I did that to you but I had to do something to make the break between us. I love you. I am yours whenever you want me. Come to the bar or back to the house. Or call and I'll come get you from wherever you are. With that said, be clear, I want you to be happy. Even if it's not with me."

He roared off, not waiting for her to leave. He knew she would be okay because Brookes and Willis were probably looking out as soon as they heard the motorcycle.

She sat in her car and cried for the longest time. She was crying for what had happened at Mike's house that was so unexpected and unnerving; crying for the loss of a friend; crying because she would definitely miss Brookes and Willis, they were like family; and crying because now she didn't have FEAST to go to for relaxing and socializing.

Brookes wanted to come out to her but Willis stopped him. She knew Pat needed to take this emotional journey alone.

CHAPTER THIRTY-FIVE

When Pat walked into the house, Robert was sitting in the dark at the kitchen island with his hands folded in front of him.

"Where have you been Pat? It is almost midnight and you have not answered my calls. I've been worried about you." His voice was cold and his words calculated.

"I'm sorry. I was at FEAST and just lost track of time. They had a birthday party in the restaurant and it was so noisy that I couldn't hear my phone."

"And what else?" he asked. "What are you not telling me?"

"What do you mean? Like what?"

"Like why you've been crying. And why your body chemistry has changed. You smell different."

Pat did not want to lie to her husband so she told him as much of the truth as she could and keep Mike from getting hurt or killed.

"Mike told me he loved me but since he knows I love you he just asked that I not come to the bar anymore."

"So why were you crying? Mike told you he loved you in my face at his house. Then I told you Mike loved you when you came home from his house. You should have never gone back." He was pissed and felt disrespected. Again.

"You're right. I just thought we could be friends. And since I always sit with Brookes and Willis, I don't even see him much when I'm there so I didn't think me going there would matter."

"Did you sleep with him?" Robert's voice was tense.

"No. Of course not!" Pat was stunned that he asked, and a little angry that he was questioning her fidelity to him after all they had been through.

"Did you want to? Never mind, do not answer that. I am going to bed. I think you need to sleep in one of these other rooms until you are done crying over your relationship with your friend." His tone was mean and snide.

"What? You don't want me anymore?" She had an attitude, almost daring him to say anything to give her a reason to leave.

"I love you Pat. I always want you. But I don't want you to bring another man into our home and definitely not into our bedroom. So take a few days to get him out of your system or 'compartmentalize' him and then come back to our bed."

"A few days? You said we could not go to bed angry or with unresolved issues. So why is tonight different? I didn't do anything wrong. I was just late and I already apologized."

"Well tonight will be the exception, so sweet dreams my wife, my love." He slammed the door to their bedroom and she heard the lock turn. Her heart actually stopped for a moment. That had never happened before.

Pat went into the guest room with the furniture from her apartment and took a long shower. Instead of sleeping, she went out onto the sunroom to think about all that had happened tonight and decide what to do next.

First, she needed to figure out how she felt about Mike kissing her and caressing her breasts. He has skills that is for sure. She probably should have been appalled and angry but she wasn't. She knew how he felt about her and she should not have put herself in that situation. She was wrong and sorry for that. But she had to admit he definitely has skills.

Mike had said something intriguing: that there was a sensual itch in her that had not been scratched. Was that true? Was that why she had such vivid, sexy dreams? Why she couldn't be mad at him for what he did? Was there something missing in her sex life with Robert? Did she need Robert to find that core in her and explore it? Would that be a turnoff to him?

She thought back over the few times she had sex with a 'bad boy.' She couldn't think of anything he had done that was different from any other man except there was an air of danger and even a little roughness that the average man didn't provide. Truth be told, it was a turn on when you knew you were with someone who cared about you and who would not hurt you. Pat had seen Roberts's adventurous side and his mean side a few times, but his rough side only when they had been a part from each other for a long time.

Did she want Mike instead of Robert? Mike was handsome and sexy for sure, and had the bad boy/roughneck attitude. And yes, she was curious and kind of attracted to him like that. But Robert brought the Panther Heat and it was still between them to this day and through the bad times. That was why she went into such a tailspin during tax season. She was hurt by him, but still wanted him, and was hopeful that they could make it through the next few months. She was glad that he was still feeling The Heat for her and came to Mike's house to get her.

She was also puzzled about why Robert had the nerve to be angry with her after the way he had ignored her. What was a couple of hours late versus weeks and weeks of being ignored?

Pat heard the sliding door to the porch open and knew Robert was standing in the doorway in the dark. She turned to look at him but neither of them spoke. Finally, she broke the silence.

"I did not cheat on you Robert. This is still a new life for me here in Dallas and writing is such a solitary profession. I don't have many friends here and I enjoyed hanging out at FEAST. So I will not go there anymore and will find other places to meet people. But I need you to trust me. It's the same trust that I have to have for you. You are a very handsome and sexy man and women are always all over you. Remember, I have seen the faces of women you have been with and who want you. I know you always leave them wanting more. They will always come for you. Are you strong enough, are we strong enough, for you to always say no to them?

"Every day when you leave here I worry that some new woman might catch your eye and you will want to get to know her. Or you will see someone who makes you want to have sex with her. You have no idea how that terrifies me, especially when you forget about me so easily."

He never commented but in his mind, he didn't believe her story about the evening. He was feeling anxious because except for being at Mikes, she had never been out late without him and he wondered who had captured her attention and made her forget to check her phone. Or check the time and just come home. Pat was a beautiful, charming woman and a lot of men probably wanted to talk to her. He knew a wedding ring would not stop a man from trying to get her attention. They were working on their relationship and were overall in a good place, he thought, so he didn't believe she would have a reason to let some other man talk to her, but who knows? He had hurt her deeply. Maybe she just needed someone else to flirt with her and flatter her, even if just for a night. He now understood very clearly how she felt when he did not come home from work and give her attention during tax season. He needed her and her attention and missed both tonight.

Finally, Pat turned her head away. She heard the door close so she figured he had gone back inside. Instead, he walked over to the sofa she was on and sat down, pulling her into his arms. They eventually laid back and she fell asleep on his chest without saying anything else.

CHAPTER THIRTY-SIX

Tax season started off quiet like the previous year. For Christmas and New Year's they spent a lot of private time together again, playing fantasy nights. He wanted them to make love on or in each one of the cars and see her in different sexy outfits each night so they could role play being naughty. She was still having reservations about tax season so she focused on indulging his fantasies. Maybe she would share hers another time.

Robert's hours expanded in January but he was true to his promise: he came home by eight each night and only worked four hours on Saturday. This time he called her every day and kissed her when he got home, and she got his attention all day on Sunday because he was not so exhausted.

They went to brunch for Valentine's Day. The afternoon was going well when two gentlemen came in and walked toward the section of the room where Robert and Pat were seated. They were busy eating and didn't notice the gentlemen until they stopped at the table.

Robert saw who it was and nodded his head. Pat looked up into Mike's eyes and they both smiled. He winked at her saying "Hello Lush." Mike asked, glancing at Robert then back at Pat, "How's everybody?"

Pat thought it was nice to see him and see him smiling at her, especially after their last time together. "Hey you. I didn't think you were allowed to eat anywhere except FEAST."

"Oh no," he said casually, looking at Robert, "got to stay on top of the competition. Have a good day." With that, the men walked away.

Robert was immediately ready to go. He didn't want Pat to think too hard about Mike and the past and flashback to the hurt that caused her to go to Mike's house. They headed for the door and she waved goodbye to Mike and his friend. Robert whispered in her ear, "And for the record, I think you're luscious too." Pat was glad she was walking in front of him so he couldn't see her blush. She thought to herself, 'My husband. Always watching, always listening, and always knowing.' She also realized that Mike's presence was a reminder to Robert that Pat had an option, a really good option, for a man, maybe even a husband, to keep Robert from getting forgetful again or too comfortable in their relationship.

Robert was thinking that Mike would always be a shadow in their lives, but he was confident enough that he could live with that. Mike had proven to be an ally when Pat was staying at his house. He had helped convince her to go back home to Robert. If Mike had not loved Pat for his own benefit, Robert could see them being friends. But Mike did love her, so he and Pat had to stay away from each other. This was a new twist for him. Robert never cared so much for a woman that competing with another man was even on his radar. He didn't think he had to compete as much as be mindful that Mike loved Pat, and Pat was feeling a strong 'friendship' with Mike that could not be ignored. Then Robert smiled as he remembered that for Pat, he had Panther Heat. That overshadowed everything else that made Mike attractive. He was eager to get home and remind his wife of that heat between them.

CHAPTER THIRTY-SEVEN

In March, Robert announced to Pat that he had been scheduled for a special assignment and was leaving before tax season was over. "They will not give me much notice and I need for us to be in a good place whenever I leave. Tell me, how are you feeling now? Are we ok?" He shared with her, "I can tell that you are still hurting from before but I had hoped that you could see that this tax season was different, better. One day I want to see the light shining in your eyes for me again." She responded, "I'm trying Robert."

They were barely settled in bed a couple of weeks later when he got "The Call." Three quick pings on his phone signaled the launch of the 'special assignment.' It was two a.m. and they were picking him up in one hour.

"Well I'm glad this tax season has been much better than last year so we could be in a good place when I leave. I couldn't function and be focused on my job if I was mad at you or if you were upset with me." He reminded her that he could not be in communication with her but that did not mean he was ignoring her or had forgotten about her. He had to be focused. She assured him that they were definitely in a better place this tax season.

Pat's heart was beating hard and fast but she put on a very brave face. She would not let his last memory of her, God forbid, be one of attitude or anger.

She smiled and asked him if he wanted a little 'middle of the night Magic' before he left to hold him while he was away. He said yes, but he only had fifteen minutes then he had to get ready. They were done in ten. When you have been together long enough, foreplay is nice, very nice, but sometimes you just have to go directly to what works and be done.

He showered and packed and she sat on the side of the bed watching and asking if she could do anything to help. He said, "No. Just sit there and be beautiful for me." Then he added, "You know I've never had a woman see me off or waiting for me after an assignment. This is interesting. Feels good though." He had to ask to be sure, "You will be here when I come back right? I still have this fear that I will come home one day and you would be gone and the house empty again."

She didn't deny that she still had several thoughts of leaving him. But tax season was better this time so she looked him in his eyes and promised him that she would be there when he came back. "I always keep my promises Robert. I'll be here." The light in her eyes still wasn't back, but he believed her and was excited to get her assurance.

He gave her instructions. "Call Shelly and let her know that I had to go away but I'll be back as soon as I can. Call Howard and Frank and tell them the same thing. They will know that I am going to be gone for a while.

"You need to know that I asked Howard and Frank to check on you if I ever go on a special assignment so you might get a call from them. I know you are strong and very independent, but it will make me feel like I'm still protecting you if I know that they are making sure you're okay. Frank and I did the same thing for Yvonne when Howard went away.

"If you get scared or lonely, call Yvonne or Shelly. You and Yvonne are close friends so I'm sure she'll be here for you. Or go to Houston and stay with Shelly and Tommy and TJ. They will understand what's going on and you will not have to explain anything to your family. Just call this number to tell the bureau where you are in case they need to get in touch with you for me, and they will let me know where you are." He left a card on the bedside table.

"If anything happens to me and you get that knock on the door and the officials are there to tell you that I am dead, I want you to call Howard and Frank and get one or both of them over here before those guys leave." The way he said it was so matter of fact, no emotion, like he had already shifted to work mode, leaving his humanity at home.

"Okay. I will do that" Pat nodded in response.

Then he said, "And one last thing. I hate to say this but I have given this a lot of thought. If something does happen to me, I want you to be with Mike."

Pat's eyes got big and she couldn't believe what she heard. "What? Are you serious? Why Mike? I thought you didn't want me around him anymore?"

"I don't. Not as long as I'm alive. And I plan for that to be a long time. But if I'm not, I need to be sure that you have someone around you who really loves you and will watch over you and care for you and love you like I do. There are a lot of guys out here who will pretend to love you just to try to get your money. I know Mike has his own and he already loves you and wants to take care of you. Besides, I know you have a little thing for him. It's okay, because I know you are mine and not going anywhere. But if …"

Pat cried out, "You're coming back Robert. Don't talk like that."

They prayed together, asking God to grant Robert favor and protection from harm and danger and bring him back home in one piece, healthy and whole. Then they asked God to give her strength to get through each day in prayer and thanksgiving that Robert will be home again soon.

In one hour sharp a car pulled up and Robert got the signal on his phone again, three quick pings. They hugged, kissed, and said, "I love you" then he told her to stay in bed.

As soon as the front door closed, she walked to the window and watched him get in and drive away in a big black SUV with the windows all blacked out.

She immediately put on the pajama bottom and t-shirt he had just gotten out of, then held his pillow for the rest of the night so she could smell as much of him as possible for as long as possible. No matter what their situation was, how much she hurt, she still loved Robert and enjoyed his closeness and smell.

In the morning, Pat called Shelly and she asked Pat to come stay with them, at least through this first time. Pat said no, thanks. She wanted to be home whenever Robert came back. Shelly then asked that she please call anytime day or night to her or Tommy if she needed them.

Next she called Howard and he told Frank. They said call them anytime day or night if she needed help with anything or a shoulder to lean on. Howard said he would tell Yvonne so she would be available too, in case she needed anything. The brotherhood was on alert and ready.

She decided to journal about this experience to help her get through it. Writing the notes on what she did and how she felt each day would give her a way to focus and keep herself in check, being strong as she promised Robert she would be.

CHAPTER THIRTY-EIGHT

The first week felt like the week he went to Quantico, only he didn't call. Pat maintained her regular schedule of exercise and writing and reading. She was glad for the alone time so she could assess their relationship. Calls to her girls in Houston and Chicago kept her distracted throughout the week. Laila always had crazy stories about the men in her life, and Yolanda was the calm voice of reason through Laila's storms. Yolanda also kept Pat up to date with news about what was going on at the college where they both taught. Sherry and Linda were friends from elementary school so they had lots of stories to reminisce about and keep Pat up to date on past classmates and laughing at some of the things they used to get into. Plus they were online dating so the stories of being mismatched were endless.

Shelly called her every day. "Just checking in," she would say. "You good?"

Pat's response was always, "I'm good."

"Okay, talk to you next time." Some time she would ask for specifics on her day to gauge her state of mind.

Yvonne called every evening and reported to Howard who reported to Frank the next day. She planned that on

Saturdays they would be together until Robert came back, either going out, depending on Pat's mood, or just staying in to watch movies or talk. Howard, Frank, and Yvonne were afraid if they all showed up or called too often it would upset her, making her think that they knew something about Robert.

The first Saturday Yvonne and Pat went shopping. They were gone all day and had a ton of fun. With her, Pat could relax because she knew what Pat was going through and didn't stare at her or ask how she was doing every five minutes.

Over the week-end Pat talked to family and when they asked, told them that Robert was fine, just working a lot. On Sunday she live streamed Wheeler Avenue Baptist Church because Tommy was preaching again, then watched several other sermons on *YouTube*. She wanted a good dose of scripture and message to help keep her uplifted and assured in her faith that staying with him was the right thing to do and that he was coming home alive and well.

The second week was like the first, but it was difficult to sleep through the nights. She always put the alarm on so she didn't think anyone would break in. The insomnia was back.

Shelly told her stories of how their mother helped them cope through the years when their dad was away for an extended period. She would have them read a number of books to show to their dad that they had been good and productive, or they planned their next birthday party, or she invited their cousins over to spend time with them and keep them distracted.

Yvonne came on Saturday and they went out riding through different neighborhoods, helping Pat get to know more areas of the city and looking at the beautiful houses.

Week three was tough. According to Frank, most assignments only lasted a couple of weeks so three was a stretch She went through the motions each day but with less and less energy. The world seemed to slow down for her. Yvonne told Howard how she was feeling and a new plan to look out for her was put in place.

Frank came on Mondays and brought dinner and told her about his adventures with women from the weekend. He was a good storyteller and his stories were funny. She needed the laughs. He always asked about Vickie. Pat reminded him that Vickie was not like the others so he needed to decide if he was ready for her.

Howard came over on Thursday morning of week four to see if everything was okay with Pat and with the house. He said as long as Robert was away he would come over on Thursdays to check on her and see if any repairs were needed on the house that he could plan to do over the weekend.

On Friday morning at six the phone rang. She didn't recognize the voice at first. He was brief: "Patricia?" he asked to verify who he was speaking with.

"Yes."

"I have a message for you. It is as follows: Good Morning Sunshine. I love you." He paused for a second then said, 'It's all good Sis.'" He hung up quickly without waiting for a comment. She realized that the man on the phone was Dexter and he was either with Robert or had spoken to him to know what to say to make her know that the message was real. No one else knew that Robert woke her up with those words. Knowing that he was okay renewed her energy.

Pat realized that she truly missed her husband and life without him would be no life for her and started praying for him to come back. She even bought him the male version of the necklace he had given her for her birthday and had it inscribed like hers: "You are my life. Love, Pat." To her, that was a symbol of their forever connection. It would be his birthday present since she had just come home from Mike's on his last birthday and did not have a gift for him.

Shelly was the first call Pat made and they cried tears of joy together.

Then Pat called Yvonne. She was happy and Howard said he was surprised she got a call. He didn't say anything to Pat, but he knew that for Robert to be gone so long, he was on a dangerous mission. The longer he was gone, the more danger he was in. Howard began to worry about his brother.

Pat called Laila and Yolanda in Houston and convinced them to take a road trip. She needed some laughs and hugs and good drinks. They came early on Saturday, and when they saw the pictures of 'Roberts's friends from work' picked Elliott and Dexter as the guys they wanted to meet as soon as it could be arranged. They thought Frank looked too much like a player. Yvonne and Pat both laughed.

She was riding high throughout week four. Very productive.

Another call came on Wednesday night at 11p.m. of week five.

Like the first call the voice said "Patricia? I have a message for you. It is as follows: Sweet dreams my wife, my love, my everything." A pause, then "We're good Sis." Click. She knew Elliott's voice. She hoped that all three of them were together, protecting each other.

Pat decided then that she could make it the rest of the time he was gone. God knew exactly what she needed and she got it. Blessings and favor would get her through the rest of the time and he was coming home alive. She just needed to be patient.

There were so many times Pat missed her mom, but this time in her life especially made Pat want to talk to her about Robert and how she fully understood what she meant about Panther Heat and loving her father so much and how no other love existed for her. She prayed that she knew and maybe would even come to her in a dream so she could give her a big hug and say thanks.

CHAPTER THIRTY-NINE

On Thursday, May 8th, the morning of week six, at about one a.m. Pat heard a car pull up. It was an unusual sound on their street at the late hour so she looked out the window and there it was, the big black SUV with the blacked out windows. Robert got out then reached back in for his bag. He took a moment to look at the house then came quietly through the front door.

Pat was back in bed, holding his pillow, crying quietly and thanking God when he came into the bedroom. He didn't say a word but came to the side of the bed and rubbed the tears from her face then smiled at her hugging his pillow. He was not ready to talk yet.

He went to the shower and stood there for a good ten minutes, arms outstretched to the walls and leaning, letting the water wash over him. Pat wanted to run in there with him but realized he needed this time to re-orient himself to being home. She waited patiently for him.

He came out of the bathroom wearing his usual pajama bottoms and a t-shirt and smelling great, like the day she met him and every day since. He now had a full-grown beard. It looked good on him, but she did not want him to keep it. Too much of a reminder of when and how he got it.

He stood at the foot of the bed and threw the cover and pillow to the side. She was wearing one of his t-shirts and nothing else.

He held her legs together at the ankles, then starting at her feet gave her butterfly kisses all the way up her legs and hips and across her stomach, between her breasts and on her shoulders and neck.

He was not trying to make love. It was more than that. He just wanted to love on her with his heart. It was the most intimate feeling Pat had ever experienced.

When he got to her face he looked into her eyes for what seemed like a long time but it was probably just a minute. His eyes had a vacant look about them and Pat felt like he was searching hers for the key to unlock the door to his soul. He had closed it off to survive.

Tears welled up in his eyes and she gave him the kisses he usually gave her: forehead, nose, cheeks, then wiped his tears and kissed his eyes.

He was trembling so she wrapped her body around his and pulled the cover over them. No talking. Just holding each other super tight. They drifted off to sleep.

CHAPTER FORTY

At 6am sharp the alarm went off. Robert woke Pat up to "Good morning Sunshine" and she smiled at him saying, 'Good morning husband'. It was the first time she had said that to him in a long time. He got excited but didn't want to assume too much too fast.

He called Shelly saying "Hey Sis" like it was just another day. Pat could hear her crying and saying how much she loved him. He promised that they would come up on Saturday for their birthday but had to come home on Sunday so he could get back to work. He needed to see her as much as she needed to see him.

He called Howard and Frank and told them he would see them Monday. Howard assured him that they had looked out for his wife but she was a trooper. Robert thanked them and called Yvonne to thank her for being with Pat every week. He promised them all that he would find the best restaurant in town for a reunion celebration.

After breakfast he asked Pat how she was doing. Really doing. He looked in her eyes and noticed something different. They weren't so cold and distant. Was she feeling sorry for him or was she beginning to love him fully again?

She admitted that it got hard, but she kept the faith. She told him about her journal and how good it was to have Yvonne, Howard, Frank, and of course, Shelly, give her so much love. And the messages really helped.

She asked how he was doing, really doing and he said, "as long as I get to be with you, I'm always great." He was sitting at the island so she walked over to him and stood between his legs and put her arms around him, hugging him tight. It was her way of saying 'You're back. I'm back with you. We're good. I love you.' He knew exactly what she was saying without her using words so he hugged her tight and whispered, "I love you. I missed you. Thank you for coming back to me." They kissed like it was the day she signed the marriage license, slow, probing, a longing for each other that was always there. She finally gave him the necklace that matched the one he had given her the year before. He put it on right away. Now all was right with her world.

They spent the day and evening in the family room. He had a bunch of calls to return so Pat went into the office and pretended to work. But she was too excited that he was home and kept going back to the family room to look at him. When he saw her he would hold his arms open for her to come to him and she would lay across his lap with her head on his chest, listening to his heartbeat while he talked. After a few minutes, she would to go back to the office or to the kitchen to get something to drink then return to the family room. This went on for about an hour, then she just stayed in the room with him, laying on the end of the sofa. She did not want to listen in on his conversations or rush him off the phone. She just wanted to look at him. She was so happy he was home and she could see him. He felt the same way and would look at her and smile and wink while he talked.

Finally, he was done with his calls so they could spend the rest of the day together. They sat holding each other while they watched television and they would fall asleep. They were both exhausted but did not want to be too far away from each other.

Pat could tell it would take him a few days to feel completely at home again, and going to Houston was an important part of getting to that feeling. They arrived super early on Saturday morning. He and Shelly hugged for the longest time in the family room so Tommy and Pat went to the kitchen to give them privacy. Tommy said he didn't know what Shelly would do if something happened to Robert and he didn't want to find out.

When TJ woke up, he heard familiar voices and ran down the stairs. He was happy to see Robert and Pat and hugged them both. Robert told him it was family day this time and they would have their day on the next visit. TJ was fine with that. He liked hanging out with the whole family.

Shelly picked the restaurant. They went back to the one where they celebrated their birthday two years before, the night they all met. *Willie G's*. It was a good choice in Pat's mind, almost like a reset, a do-over, to that time when meeting each other was fresh and new but better now because they were a solid and complete family. They all relaxed and just focused on being together again.

Conversation flowed with updates from TJ about school, episodes from work from Shelly, and Tommy's job and events at Wheeler.

CHAPTER FORTY-ONE

On the ride back to Dallas Pat asked Robert, "Do you feel different when you're on a special assignment with a wife now versus before when you were single? Did your demeanor change while you were away?"

He responded slowly. "I did notice that I was a bit more cautious and definitely more concerned with getting back safely and quickly."

She then asked, "How important are the special assignments to you now? Do you need them to feel good about your career and accomplishments or could you do without them?"

He liked that she asked and responded earnestly, "It was on my mind on the trip home. I decided that I can do without the special assignments. I have given enough of myself to the bureau and now I want to give all of my time to you and to our being together."

Pat then raised the question of whether there was any way he could get out of the missions and just go to Quantico an extra week or two each year. She couldn't imagine going through any weeks like what she had just experienced again, especially if they had kids. His mom was a better woman that Pat thought she could ever be.

He promised to work on that as soon as he got to the office the next day.

First thing Monday morning Pat noticed that Robert's eyes were back to normal, warm and focused on her. He also let her know that the Python was awake and asking for her. It was an intense reunion of their bodies, slow and focused and sensual, like it was their first time together. They kissed a long time, reacquainting themselves with each others tongues and taste and smell and soft spots that made them moan. Robert's hands were more firm on Pat's body, a sign that he missed her and that he needed to hold her tight to confirm that he was finally back home. He needed to be sure the Panther Heat was still working for them and that he could make her body cry so his lips found their way to her breasts and stomach and thighs and his juice box. With no condom in the way, they sealed themselves together and rode slowly like they were on the slow train to nowhere. No stops. No destination. They both needed to feel the pressure, the heat, the fire that had kept them connected for six weeks. They both wept tears of joy to be together again and resumed their Morning Magic, only slower and more intense every day.

The following week-end Robert made good on his promise of dinner at a five star restaurant for Howard, Yvonne, and Frank. Frank did not want to bring a date, saying it was family night. Everyone appreciated that sentiment and had a grand time, talking about everything that had happened over the six weeks, but never addressing the impact of Robert's absence on each of them individually. You could tell by the look in everyone's eyes that Robert was special to each of them for their own reasons and they were all grateful for his return.

Robert had his moments too. As conversation flowed, he looked at each person very intently, not really listening as much as looking, loving being surrounded by family. Just before dessert he stood up abruptly and went to the men's room, coming back with red eyes. He and Howard and Frank looked at each other and in that unspoken language of the brotherhood, Howard and Frank communicated 'We know. But it's all good now.' You could see Robert relax and he finally smiled. Now all was right with his world.

Robert's love was steadfast from day one. Pat finally felt comfortable and at home forever with the love of her life, the man who brought the Panther Heat. Yes, she would take that leap again. Mom was right. Panther Heat really is the best kind of love.

QUESTIONS FOR DISCUSSION

1. Robert and Patricia met and married on the same day. Is this something you would or could do? Why or why not? Do you know anyone who has done that or something similarly quick? How long did their relationship last?

2. Robert says he is celibate. Do you believe a handsome Black man with many women who want him could be celibate? Have you ever personally known any Black man to be celibate? If so, why did they decide to do that?

3. Patricia and Robert both came from loving two-parent households and wanted the same for themselves. Is that your reality? If not, how do you think your perspective on love and romance has been shaped by being raised in a single parent household?

4. Did Patricia make too much of the way Robert 'dismissed' her when Lynnette made her announcement about having Robert's child?

5. Did Patricia overreact to Robert's long hours at work after promising to be understanding and strong?

How do you handle your partner's long work hours? Have you ever felt lonely and unappreciated? What would you do if you did feel lonely and unappreciated? Have you ever or would you cheat on him/her?

6. Was Patricia cheating on Robert with an emotional relationship with Mike? Was she cheating because she always let him pay for her food and drinks whenever she was at FEAST? What would you have done to resist Mike's charms?

7. Where would you have gone at the end of tax season to wait for the divorce papers to be signed and delivered? Would you have gone to Mikes? If not, where else? Or stayed at home?

8. Did Patricia overreact when she got the video of her husband Eric with the two women? Have you ever had someone send you a video of your mate with another or other people? What did/would you do?

9. Did you or anyone you know grow up in the social welfare system like Frank? What was it like? Did/could it make you jaded and not want a relationship?

10. In speaking with Yvonne about Eric, Patricia asked, "Why do women do that all the time—blame themselves instead of seeing the man for who he really is?" Do you or anyone you know do that? What's the reason (or reasons)?

# # #

ABOUT THE AUTHOR

Pam Kelly spent her teen years on Chicago's South Side reading romance novels and watching her parents live out their own real life love story. After earning two masters degrees and having a successful career in advertising, she went from studying brands to studying the magic and nuance of relationships – her own and others-- and now writes about them in sensual romance novels. Her characters are bold and strong, flawed and sensitive, and all kinds of sexy. Their stories are compelling, heart wrenching, and romantic.

Pam loves reading, music, decorating, a good laugh, and beautiful shoes. Her Goddaughters and nieces and their children keep her busy and up-to-date on all things new. She resides in Houston, Texas.

Connect with Pam online:
- PamelaFKelly.com
- *Facebook:* Pamela F. Kelly
- *Instagram:* Pamela.F.Kelly
- *Twitter:* @PamelaFKelly1

CPSIA information can be obtained
at www.ICGtesting.com
Printed in the USA
BVHW071918091121
621185BV00006B/353